I0549733

Justice

JUSTICE

Her Sweet Revenge Series - Book #2

Mimi Barbour

Sarna Publishing

This is a work of fiction. Names, characters, places,

and incidents are either the product of the

author's imagination or are used fictitiously,

and any resemblance to actual persons

living or dead, business establishments, events, or locales,

is entirely coincidental.

"Justice"

Her Sweet Revenge Series – Book #2

No part of this book may be used or

reproduced in any manner whatsoever

without written permission of the author except in the case

of brief quotations embodied in critical articles or reviews.

Contents

Dedication

I'm dedicating this series to my father, who we lovingly refer to as Papa John. This man has been a huge influence throughout my life. He's a smart, energetic, affectionate and very wise ninety-two-year-old man who is still going strong – likes to brag that he's only taking one pill a day. He's legally blind, but no one can tell from the way he gets around. Whenever he appears in the dining room at his lodge, people light up, and the jokes start flying.

This man brightens the day for everyone around him, and it thrills me to be his very fortunate daughter. To dedicate this new series to him is my way of telling the world that without his calm guidance and constant example, I'd never be the writer, the wife, the mother or the successful, happy woman I am today.

I love you, Papa John!

*Sadly, I lost my wonderful Papa John in 2018, and in his memory I wrote a book using him as one of the characters. It's called Special Agent Charli. So far, he seems to be reaping the best comments in the book's many reviews. Amazon Universal link: http://mybook.to/SpecialAgentCharli

Praise

"A continuation of Sweet Retaliation. The story is action-packed as we continue to learn the story of Cass's brother's death and the gang he had gotten himself involved in. Ms. Barbour knows how to draw you into a story and keep you there until the end. Now for the third book and hopefully the end of the story." ~ *Reviewed by Janine*

"As entertaining as the first book in the series. I couldn't stop reading! Very well written, compelling, and with complex characters – some of whom sometimes slink along the line of good and evil incredibly convincingly. A good bit of romance, but romance isn't the main driver of the storyline. Neither is revenge, although you'd think so from the beginning. Rather, this is a beautifully composed story of maturation, family, strength, friendship, and letting go. Can't wait for the third installment to see how Cassi's story is resolved." ~ *Reviewed by Bella*

"Most interesting book. Lots of characters, most, none we would want to meet. Second in the series, and all the main characters are there. Minor ones have come and gone. They live a gang lifestyle with drugs and guns. The good guys are doing their best to find the truth and Cassidy is pushing the bar to find out who killed her brother. Unfortunately, there are creatures plotting her downfall. Good book, good plot, great characters and now I must be patient and wait for book three."~ *Reviewed by Shirleen*

"Love this new series by Mimi. Kickass heroine, smart, sexy hero, interesting storyline equals great reading.
Fans of her Vegas series will want to get this. Those of you who haven't read a book by this author, start here. Enjoy" ~ *Reviewed by jane austen*

Also author of...

***Most of Mimi's books can be found FREE on Kindle Unlimited!!
Universal Links used for your Amazon address.
***

~*~*~*~
The Vicarage Bench Series
— Spirit Travel at its Best! —
She's Me (Book 1)
He's Her (Book 2)
We're One (Book 3)
Vicarage Bench Anthology (Book 4 – Books 1-3)
Together Again (Book 5)
Together for Christmas (Book 6)
Together Always (Book 7)
~~*

Angels with Attitude Series
— Angels Playing Cupid! —
The Angels with Attitudes Anthology (Books 1-3)
My Cheeky Angel (Book 1)
His Devious Angel (Book 2)
Loveable Christmas Angel (Book 3)
A Wonderful Life (Book 4)
Mischievous Christmas Angel (Book 5)
~~*

Elvis Series

— Make an Elvis Song a Book! —
She's Not You (Book 1)
Love Me Tender (Book 2)
~~*

Vegas Series
— Action–Packed Thrillers! —
Vegas Series – Complete Boxed Set
Partners (Book 1)
Roll the Dice (Book 2)
Vegas Shuffle (Book 3)
High Stakes Gamble (Book 4)
Spin the Wheel (Book 5)
Let it Ride (Book 6)
~~*

Undercover FBI Series
— Popular & Compelling! —
Special Agent Francesca (Book 1)
Special Agent Finnegan (Book 2)
Special Agent Maximilian (Book 3)
Special Agent Kandice (Book 4)
Special Agent Booker (Book 5)
Special Agent Charli (Book 6)
Special Agent Rylee (Book 7)
Special Agent Murphy (Book 8)
Special Agent Sophia (Book #9 – to be released
in May 2020)
~~*

Holiday Heartwarmers Series
— Truly a Christmas favorite! —
Holiday Heartwarmers Trilogy

Please Keep Me (Book 1)
Snow Pup (Book 2)
Find Me a Home (Book 3)
Frosty the Snowman (Book 4)
Love of my Life (Book 5)
A Perfect Storm (Book 6)
~~*

Her Sweet Revenge Series
— She's unstoppable! —
Retaliation (Book #1)
Justice (Book #2)
Resolution (Book #3)
Endings – (Book #4)
Faith (Book #5)
Leni (Book #6)
~~*

Single Title Series
He's My Baby (Book #1)
Christmas Runaway (Book #2)
Because You cared (Book #3)
Daddy's Mine (Book #4)
~~*

The Best in Romance Series
Red Hot Divas (Book #1 Box Set)
Hot and Handsome (Book #2 Box Set
~~*

Other Titles
I'm No Angel
Hotshot Cowboy
Big Girls Don't Cry

Christmas Runaway

The Surrogate's Secret

Mimi's Mix (Box Set)

'Tis the Season (Box Set)

Hearts, Flowers & Romance (Box Set)

Love, Christmas (Multi-author Box Set)

Unforgettable Romances (Multi-author Box Set)

Sweet and Sassy (Multi-author Box Set)

Unforgettable Heroes (Multi-author Box Set)

Unforgettable Christmas (Multi-author Box Set)

A Christmas She'll Remember (Multi-author Box Set)

Snowflakes and Christmas Kisses (Multi-author Box Set)

Unforgettable Valentine (Multi-author Box Set)

A Valentine She'll Remember (Multi-author Box Set)

Unforgettable Suspense (Multi-author Box Set)

Unforgettable Danger (Multi-author Box Set)

Unforgettable Trouble (Multi-author Box Set)

Unforgettable Weddings (Multi-author Box Set)

A Wedding She'll Remember (Multi-author Box Set)

Sweet and Sassy Brides (Multi-author Box Set)

Love, Christmas 2 (Multi-author Box Set)

Sweet and Sassy Suspense (Multi-author Box Set)

Unforgettable Thrills (Multi-author Box Set)
Unforgettable Passion (Multi-author Box Set)
A Romance She'll Remember (Multi-author
Box Set)
Sweet and Sassy Cinderella (Multi-author Box
Set)
Unforgettable Power (Multi-author Box Set)
Daring Protectors (Multi-author Box Set)
Unforgettable Charmers (Multi-author Box Set)
Sweet and Sassy Baby Love (Multi-author Box
Set)
Sweet and Sassy Heroes (Multi-author Box Set)
Unforgettable Intrigue (Multi-author Box Set)
Unforgettable Christmas Dreams (Multi-author
Box Set)
Sweet and Sassy Holiday (Multi-author Box
Set)
Christmas Shorts (Multi-author Box Set)
Unforgettable Temptations (Multi-author Box
Set)
Doctors in Love #1 (Multi-author Box Set)
Doctors in Love #2 (Multi-author Box Set)
Cute but Crazy (Multi-author Box Set)
Sweet and Sassy Daddies ((Multi-author Box
Set)
Unforgettable Joy (Multi-author Box Set)
~~*

All Mimi's books can be found on her Amazon
Author Page:
http://bit.ly/MimiBarbourAmazon

OR

Website: http://mimibarbour.com

Chapter One

The first punch missed Cassidy Santino by a mere inch. Swift and aimed to hurt, the second rammed her mask and flung her head to the side. She blocked the follow-up jabs to her stomach with automatic reflexes. The uppercut caught her snoozing, and down she went.

The owner of Rusty's Gym in Las Vegas bellowed his disgust. "Shit, Cass, get up. What the hell is going on in your head, girl? Arlene has kicked the crap out of you for two days now, and she's enjoying it."

Rusty pointed at the smirking girl who bounced in place, her head never stopping its side-to-side movement. She was revved, and Cassi knew it.

Suddenly, he pointed to the locker area. "Okay, Arlene, you've had your fun. Enough. Hit the showers. We'll work on your jabs again tomorrow."

"Yeah, okay, boss." She slouched to leave the

ring where Rusty separated the ropes. When she landed on the floor next to him, she swiveled and added. "Maybe you should get me another sparring partner; Rus. Cass's reached her limit. She can't keep up with me anymore. Think you can find me another fighter who'll give me a workout?"

"Yeah, yeah. Even on her worst day, Cass could put you on your ass and don't you forget it, girl. Now go." His roar didn't have the same emphasis as usual, and both girls heard the lack of conviction.

Still sitting on the canvas flooring, arms over her knees and her head bent, Cass didn't care what the other said. The insults didn't matter. Nothing mattered.

Detective Trace Maguire hadn't called.

And, he'd ignored all her attempts to contact him.

No doubt, disgusted and fed up with her stubborn plans for revenge on who murdered her brother, he'd left her. And she couldn't blame him.

Alone and more afraid than she'd ever been, the emptiness mocked and the voices inside her head never stopped with the name-calling. *Fool! Idiot! Dumb-ass!* However, her intentions of finding her brother's killer hadn't and wouldn't change. Nothing would stop her, not even Trace's abandonment.

Didn't mean her heart wasn't breaking though. Or, that hell might be more fun than her life without him. Her trainer's loud grumblings cut into her brooding and forced an answer.

"I'm sorry, Rusty. I'm not concentrating. I'll be on top of things tomorrow."

"Shit, girl, you'd better be. Arlene has a big fight coming up this weekend, and she's too dam confident for my liking. If she goes into the ring feeling like this, that bitch she's up against will wipe the floor with her. You gotta make her work harder. It's why you're here. We need you."

"I know." Shocked at her loudness, Cass lowered her voice to admit, "I just don't care."

"Well, any stupid blind fool can see that." Rusty moved into the ring and plunked himself down beside her on the floor. "What's up, little girl? You look like you've lost your best friend. Is it still Raoul's dying? Has it finally hit you? I've heard some people have these weird relapses a while after their loved ones have passed. You know – it becomes real."

"It's not that, Rusty. I've accepted that Raoul's gone." She removed her mask and began working on her gloves.

Rusty grabbed her hands and took over the chore. "Then what the freakin' hell has got you mooning around like a lovesick fool?" He glowered at her. Then his scruffy face took on a knowing look, and he bristled. "Okay, kiddo. Who is he?" Rusty's one good eye seared through her response, and she couldn't pretend. "Lord-love-a-duck, please tell me it's not that young idiot, Juan Acedo.

That guy's dumb as a stump. Talk about a patsy in the ring. Hell, I could whip the shit outta him. And I'm twice his age."

Cass arched her eyebrow at Rusty, and a playful look appeared. "You mean three times."

He grinned in acknowledgment and then bristled. "Don't you mess with me, girl. I'm worried aboutcha." Rusty put his arm around her shoulder and gave her a little shake.

Cass let her head rest on his hand for a moment and lifted it before he became uncomfortable. "No. I don't even like Juan. Most times, he gives me the creeps. Never mind, Rusty. I'll get over it. Tomorrow, I'll come prepared and it'll be better."

A shadow stepped into the light, a male who she knew very well. Cassi waved a greeting at the newcomer. "Hey, Sam. You looking for me?"

Sam Smith, the bartender at the Lipstick Club where Cassidy worked, leaned over the ropes while he grinned down at the pair on the floor. "Just coming to see how you are, Cass. Seems to me if you can box, your hand must be better after slugging the dude at the raid the other night. Figure you can come back to the bar and help me again? I'm fed up working with the idiots Rodrigo hired as temps."

Rusty stiffened. Cass figuratively rolled her eyes and glared at Sam. She saw his grin and knew he'd purposely put her on the hot seat. Before she could make little of his comments, Rusty's temper kicked in, and he swiveled her way.

"What the hell's he talking about? That's not what you told me, Cass. I want the truth young lady. Now."

"Sam's making it sound bad, and he wasn't even there." Cass growled the last few words in the culprit's direction and got another grin for her trouble. "I stumbled on a police raid at a drug house, and a little girl was imprisoned in her mama's car—"

"A little girl? What the hell was a kid doing at a drug house?"

"Her mother drove into the driveway to buy drugs just as the police arrived and all hell broke loose. I saw what was going down. Got the little darling out, and when one of the sicko's wanted to use her as a negotiating tool, we had a skirmish. I hit him. Hurt my hand a bit. No biggie."

"And you didn't tell me this – why?"

She arched her brow and waited without saying a thing.

"Don't be cute, brat. You and me, we're family. You don't play silly games with me." His tone meant business, and Cassidy felt remorse crawl over her and let him see it. "You're right, Rus. From now on, I'll behave." She hoped he didn't realize her words were chosen with care. She hadn't promised, not to lie because being truthful wasn't her way anymore.

Chapter Two

Once she changed, Cass and Sam left the gym together.

"You up for a cup of coffee, Sweetheart?"

"Don't you sweetheart me, Sam Smith. You set me up in there with Rusty. Why?"

Innocence didn't sit well on the pony-tailed, biker-looking guy whose lanky tallness, all-seeing gaze and middle-age looks never deceived her. He had scanners in the back of his head, knew what went on at the bar at all times and had turned into a friend. At least, she thought he had. After today, she wasn't too sure.

"Calm down, chick. I was just messin' with you. Come on now; don't be mad at old Sam. After all, I'm the one who's covering your shifts, ain't I?"

Cass slipped her fingers into his and started in the direction of the nearest coffee place. "Yeah, yeah." She grinned inwardly at how much she sounded like Rusty. "You've been a real peach."

Soon they were settled at a table, each with

coffees and a piece of apple pie. Sam opened the conversation. "I heard about the bust and what went down at the bakery, kid. Tough shit to deal with. You sure you're okay? I could hang on for a few more days if you need the time."

"Nah! I was coming in tonight anyway, sent you a text. Guess you didn't get it." Cass lowered her eyes before adding the rest. "I need to get back to work, Sam. It's been impossible to sleep just replaying what happened that night."

"First of all, no one knows you were there except a couple of cops, and the dude you took down. He made you for an undercover and refuses to talk so you're clear. Between you and me, I can't imagine how you got involved."

Cass thought over his words and knew there was a disconnect staring her in the face. Suddenly it hit her. "Hey, if no one else knows about it, how come you do?"

Sam grinned. "Your pick-up driver, Detective Maguire, enquired about you, and in confidence, he mentioned the circumstances of why you mightn't be back to work for a while. Maguire looked like he'd eaten a pound of lemons, the poor sucker. Sour as all get-out."

"He asked about me?" Cass's heart tripped, then sped up.

"Not really. I figure he came in to bitch about your involvement."

"I explained it all to him after it happened.

Tommy had confided in me about the raid, how him and some friends were going to take down the new distributor selling from the bakery on Arlington. Curious, I went there to check it out. I saw the mother heading to the place to buy drugs and warned her not to go there. Even though she had her little girl strapped into her seat in the back, the crazy woman must have been desperate. So, I followed. How could I ignore the situation? I'm glad I didn't."

"Funny thing, Detective McGuire said the same thing."

"Yeah? Well, it would be a heck of a lot more meaningful if he'd said it to me." She slid out of her chair, dropped some bills on the table and nodded to her bar-partner. "See you tonight."

Chapter Three

Sam Smith watched the slender girl's stride. Cassidy Santino had midnight black hair cut just under her ear on the right side to frame her face, a soft curtain to hide behind—one she used a lot. Whereas on the left, she'd had her head shaved. The contrast worked in her favor. She could win beauty contests.

Today, she'd worn very little makeup and looked like a schoolgirl with her soft skin and big eyes. When she wasn't acting as a hard-assed babe of the gang world, she appeared young and naïve. Slap on her party face: add the outrageous earrings she tended to wear, the colored hair sprays, the painted on tats, and she looked like a tough chick who knew the ropes.

He'd decided a while ago there were two personalities vying inside her—one, a shy, loving female who enchanted everyone with her slanted, vivid blue, South American sparklers.

The other was a secretive girl, a nobody's fool who could take care of herself and was solid. It was this Cass, who was on a quest to find her twin brother's killers. Sam hadn't yet decided which personality he liked best.

Guess it didn't matter since he'd protect her through any shit she found herself in. While doing so, he'd handle his FBI narcotics undercover assignment at the club.

His main concern, the initial source of their drugs had to be uncovered. And the monkey business happening upstairs at the club kept under surveillance and reported on. Too many young girls suddenly appeared from who knew where? Too many drugs came and left the premises and needed to be scrutinised. And a chance to catch the kingpin behind the huge distribution, kept his focus where it belonged.

Making up his mind, he sent a text. Sauntering past his table, the waitress smiled an invitation. He grinned in response. Why women were attracted to him; he'd never figured out. A girlfriend once told him it was the hint of danger and mystery that lurked around him that drew them in.

Flirting a little, he ordered another cup of coffee and one more piece of pie. Then he watched as the buxom blonde swayed over to the counter, her generous ass a picture of delight.

When Trace Maguire stepped into the place, not

only Sam watched him maneuver his way through the filled tables to slump down on the chair across from him. Most of the drooling females in the place had their eyes on him too. The man's rumpled suit, undone tie and wrinkled shirt wasn't expected attire for a Las Vegas Detective, but it made him strangely approachable.

"Hey dude. You don't look so good." Sam got a kick out of picking at sores. He knew the guy across from his was one big walking wound who appeared ready to explode.

While he waited for Trace's answer, he sussed him out and had no doubt as to why Cass had fallen for the jerk. The detective would appeal to any woman with decent vision. Trace's hard face softened by his longish dark waves was a major attraction only surpassed by striking indigo eyes that didn't miss a thing.

"Fuck you." Trace's thick eyebrow arced, a reaction that reminded Sam of who had just used the same maneuver earlier. It was obvious; Cassidy spent time with this Romeo. "What's up?" Sam forced Trace to ask the question. Why should he make it easy on the love-sick fool?

Just then the waitress arrived with a cup and a coffee pot and waited for Trace to nod in agreement before she poured. Her interest now in the newcomer, she arched her body in a suggestive stance and smiled warmly. "Want I should bring a menu, sugar?"

"Nah. This is good, thanks." When Trace didn't notice her machinations, she shrugged and moved to the next table.

Trace glared at Sam. "Don't play stupid. What did Cassidy say?"

"Exactly what you figured she would. She's back at work tonight."

"Shit!" Trace stirred sugar in his coffee, clanking the spoon against the sides of the mug—his frustration evident. "Did you tell her she could take more time?"

"Yep. Wasn't interested." Sam watched the worry escalate in Trace's expression and took pity on the man. "Her stubbornness kicked in but I caught a glimpse of regret before she hid it. The chick's suffering, Trace. Are you sure by using this stay-away tactic, it's going to make her stop what she's vowed to do?"

"I'd hoped so. Yet, I'm not surprised it backfired. All she thinks about is finding out who killed her brother and then getting revenge."

"Okay, you're the cop. Solve the mystery, and she'll back off."

Trace slapped the table so hard the spoon flipped. "What the hell do you think I've been doing? Tommy Wilkens was my only witness and Mendes killed him. Stupid rooky bastards at the jail stuck Tommy in the same area as the man whose daughters were killed by his gang. The sucker didn't last the night. Now I got nothing.

And, until I solve the mystery, Cassi has vowed vengeance. And you know as well as I do, that tenacious lady has a strange way of getting what she wants."

"I know." Sam slumped lower in his seat. "It was her who set up Tommy to take on the raid at the bakery, wasn't it? And it was her who maneuvered you to be there to catch him red-handed with your posse."

"Crissakes, man, I swear I wished Tommy was Raoul's shooter. The case would be solved, and she'd back off."

"You got him hitting the drug nest, right?"

"Yeah. But, he didn't shoot Raoul. Between you and me, as soon as I saw him, I knew Tommy couldn't have killed Raoul Santino that night behind the warehouse. Just before I ran out to pull Cassi from the line of fire, I saw the shooter. Oh, not his face. This dude appeared smaller built and shorter than average."

"Did you mention that to Cassi?"

"The less I involve her, the better." Trace scrubbed his fingers through his long hair to brush it away from his face, the same as he'd been doing since he'd arrived. He hunched over his coffee. "So, what do I do? Staying away is killing me. Yet, if anything happens to her, I'm done. Bloody women!"

Taking pity on the man in agony, Sam spoke, his soft tone taking out some of the sting. "Look, I got her covered when she's working the bar. The rest is up to you. Seems to me, the best way you can know what she's up to is by being as close to her as possible."

Trace brightened, his eyes lit with a flame that changed his whole demeanor from sad sap to a man with a purpose... a happy one. "You think so?"

Sam stood. As a habit he never broke, he surveyed the room to be sure he hadn't missed anything. He felt sure no one paid them any attention. Walking behind Trace, he slapped his shoulder and added, "Give both her and yourself a break, man. Call her. Better yet, go and see her. I don't think I can handle her tonight looking so gloomy. Poor babe acts like she lost her reason for living."

Chapter Four

Trace didn't see Sam leave. His mind focused on how he would approach Cassi and what he would say. Ever since the night of the raid when she stated she wouldn't stop her revenge against the other two people involved with killing her brother, Trace's Irish stubbornness had kicked in bigtime. For her own good, he'd decided to teach her a lesson. She needed to stop playing vigilante and he had to stop enabling her.

He'd refused her calls, disregarded her texts and ignored his sore gut and aching heart telling him that this bullshit had to stop. He groaned. How long could a guy stay away when the woman he hungered for needed him?

Fuck! Why did women have to be so friggin' hard to get along with? He pictured his mom, another female in his life who wouldn't listen to reason. She suffered from bone cancer and refused to go into a care facility that would take better care of her than what they could manage at home—even with a full-time nurse.

Thank goodness, this newest one, Mary Devin, found by Cassi through her acquaintance with Juan Acedo, seemed to have filled the spot quite admirably. The two women liked each other and knowing she was cared for gave him more freedom to give more energy to his job and carry on with his own life.

Right now, that meant renewing his relationship with Cassidy Santino. He needed to keep her safe, while using his network of resources to find Raoul Santino's murderer.

The vibration going on in his pocket gained his attention. He whipped out his phone and checked the texts. His partner Diane needed him. Jesus this city never did sleep. Here it was the middle of the day and they'd found a corpse, a guy from the same gang who'd killed Tommy Wilkens, *Los Soldados*. And so it went – never ending retaliation. You kill one of ours and we'll get even.

An older Vegas gang, the *Soldados* were the biggest rivals of the recent newcomers, the same group that Cassi's brother Raoul Santino had enlisted with, *Armas Jóvenes*. They warred over territory, drug rights, and in the end, it came down to who had the biggest set of balls.

Dani Andino, the *Armas* leader, as hard-assed as they come, ran the Lipstick Club where Cassi worked and kept a tight rein on her boys. Her power had become indisputable.

Although, in the early days, he'd heard stories about a ghost leader who'd controlled her, this person no longer appeared on the scene. Had she killed the sucker and hid the body where they'd never find it? Wouldn't put it past the lunatic. Nowadays, no one questioned her authority.

According to Sam, the crazy bi-sexual bitch liked women more than men and had her eyes on his Cassi. Jesus, Mary & Joseph! Nothing got him angrier than thinking of the red-headed, twisted-sister coming on to his lady.

Trace left a generous tip, waved at the friendly waitress and headed for his vehicle, which he'd left across the street. He drove past the Vegas strip, following directions to the back alley where his crew waited.

Parking his black SUV a block away so he could leave without being hassled, Trace made his way forward only to be stopped by a pack of young bloods angling for a fight. Though his shield sat on his waist in full view, these guys were riding their drug-induced highs, bursting with adrenalin and pissed that they'd lost another gang member.

The ugliest and toughest of the bunch blocked his path, the guy's sweaty stink repellent to Trace. Having no choice, Trace stopped and stared the guy down.

"Hey, cop, you see what they did to Normie?

They carved their letters on his chest. Bastards cut him like he wasn't even human, like a fucking slice of cheese. That bitch, Andino's cruising for an all-out-war. She wants it; we'll give it to her."

Waiting, knowing bullshit bravado when he heard it, Trace never flinched, his eye contact steady. He watched the idiot swallow and knew he'd won. "Back off, prick and let me do my job. All of you—leave now or I'll arrest you for pissing off a police officer in his line of duty and... for stinking up the streets." He pushed the ape away and added, "Go find a shower, man. You're rank." He put his hand on his weapon and didn't move. In a few seconds, they slunk away, grumbling, taking their grievances with them. He headed down the lane in no mood to put up with their crap.

Lord almighty, these kids should be in high school studying for their finals instead of some wacko's warriors, ready to die for their gangs so the leaders could live the big life.

It was all a sick story of the way the world worked today. Money and power and screw the little guy!

Chapter Five

Cass stood on the wrap-around veranda of her childhood home and acknowledged the earlier wave of trepidation that washed over her.

Thank goodness her stalker, Juan Acedo, wasn't anywhere to be seen. Today, she wasn't in any mood to play his sick games. The bushes he tended to hide behind after she'd banned him from his favorite cactus were empty.

Yet something felt wrong. Uncomfortable as hell, she unlocked the front door and stepped into the room, all her defences on high alert.

Nothing seemed out of place... except for the smell. It was faint, a distinct stench of pot hung in the air. Juan always stunk of the crap. As Cass made her way from room to room, her body tingling with anticipation; she knew he'd been in her house.

Once in her bedroom, the scent became stronger. It reeked on her smooth bed where the covers were slightly wrinkled, not at all like she'd left them that morning. Leaning over, she picked up her pillow and sure enough, someone had put their greasy hair there, leaving an odor that sickened her.

Yuck! The bastard had been in her house. She opened all her drawers and knew he'd spent time with her underwear just by the way he'd left her panties and bras crumpled rather than folded as usual.

Revulsion attacked and sickness reeled in her stomach making her eyes water. *That sicko!*

She grabbed her bedding and all of her undies and headed for the laundry room. Furious, she stuffed the works into the washer and uncaring about the outcome, she added the soap and ramped the temperature up to hot.

It was time for her to have a serious talk with the dude. No more making excuses or pretending. He couldn't be allowed to come and go as he pleased or spy on her from the road all night. She was sick and tired of putting up with his nonsense.

The more she thought about the confrontation, the stronger her head ached and her nerves became rattled. Juan Acedo might come across as being an ordinary guy, even one who loved his stepmother. But his actions weren't normal, spying and breaking into her home. The guy was unhinged and no one knew what evil a person like him could be capable of.

The only reason she'd given him so much leeway

was because of his previous loyalty to Raoul. Juan had been beaten for refusing to be involved in her brother's initiation. It happened the same night his own gang members killed her brother when he wouldn't shoot their rival, Sergio Mandalas.

Suddenly, she heard footsteps on her porch and reached into the closet to grab her brother's old baseball bat. No more nicey-nice. If Juan thought he could break into her home and mess with her things, she'd set him straight.

Tip-toeing to stand behind the door when it opened, she waited. In seconds, she heard the lock give way and watched the doorknob turn. Taking small breaths, she controlled the panic in her throat and the sobs that were desperate to escape.

She watched the space widen a few inches and held the bat shoulder high; thinking to strike after the person had stepped into the room. Time stood still. Sweat broke out on her chest and her back and her heart started hammering. Still she held her position and her breath.

It seems the person had decided to retreat rather than come inside. *What the hell?* The door closed, the lock reset and footsteps could be heard leaving. Stunned, Cassi looked down and there on the floor was a huge bouquet of pink roses dressed up with a big white and silver bow.

Trace?

She dropped the bat and raced out of the house in time to see a strange car drive away.

Chapter Six

Slow in re-entering the house, Cassi didn't know whether to be happy or scared. That hadn't been Trace's car. She knew his vehicle.

She bent to pick up the roses and hoped she'd find a card. Searching through the flowers, she pricked her finger on a sharp thorn and sucked at it.

She retrieved the little white envelope stuck into a holder in the center of the bunch and opened it with care. At first, the Happy Birthday message didn't make any sense until she realized the date. The next day was her twenty-ninth birthday.

The penned words, like those a lover would send, didn't ring true. *Love you.* Kisses and hugs followed and right at the bottom, where her fingers clenched the card, her blood stained the corner. *No Signature.* Trickles of apprehension assaulted. In reaction, she stuffed the gift in the kitchen trash.

Starring down at the beautiful blooms, she hesitated. What if Trace had sent them via a messenger?

She knew better. Still, her heart leapt. Would Trace have known about her birthday? She didn't think so. Her mind corrected her wishful thinking. It wasn't Trace, you lovesick idiot. He'd have signed the card. And he wouldn't have allowed anyone to break into her house, not for any reason.

Frustrated, she wished she'd looked to see who the person had been rather than hide the way she had. She'd know the culprit and could decide how to tackle the problem. Whoever sent her love notes needed to understand she wasn't interested.

Unless Trace decided to be reasonable, she could envision herself as a wrinkled, sour old maid. After the way he'd taken her virginity, made love to her and lifted her to heights she'd never known existed, she wanted no other man. Tears gathering, she turned away. The sounds of a car outside stopped her in her tracks.

When the bell sounded, she trudged to the door. Smart this time, she checked the window to see her visitor and her blood began pounding, making it difficult to breathe. She swiped at her eyes, ran her hands through her hair and slapped at her cheeks. Then she took a huge breath and swallowed the sob that fought to get loose.

As she opened the door, shyness overcame and she hid behind her curtain of hair to peek at him. "Hi, Trace."

"Can I come in, Cassidy?"

Stumbling backward, she swung the door wide and made room. "Sure. Of course. Yes, come in. Please."

She knew he stared but couldn't meet his gaze or her heart would be on display. The longing and hunger that battled inside ever since he'd decided to stay away would be exposed and leave her vulnerable.

Instead, she turned toward the kitchen. "Would you like a coffee? I was just about to make some for myself."

He moved in behind her and spoke, his voice husky, his need apparent. "Cassi, baby, I'm sorry. I couldn't stay away any longer. These last few days just about killed me—"

Pivoting, she flung herself toward him and clung, her own arms clamped around his neck while tears dampened his throat. "I thought you'd left me forever. You were so disappointed in me. I'm so-sorry."

"No, honey, I wasn't disappointed in you. Never in you. Only in your decision not to end your vendetta."

She stiffened—couldn't help it. Had Trace returned to start the same old arguments again? God, she hoped not. Losing him for the days he'd stayed away had devastated her. Like the end of everything worthwhile.

Her grief over Raoul's death had been deep and all-consuming. The misery Trace's absence caused had been shattering, threatening to break her fragile heart. In the end, it was Rusty's need for her help that had dragged her out of bed.

"No. Don't pull away. I didn't come here to talk about Raoul's murder, baby. I just need to hold you."

Thank God!

"I prayed you'd come back. It's been horrible without you, Trace." Her voice broke and she wriggled in closer until he lifted her into his arms. While she wrapped her legs around his waist, his hands supported her butt.

His lips devoured hers and her whimpers of need joined with his groans of approval. In no time, the kiss had spiraled out of control. He headed for her bedroom in search of comfort. Once there, he lowered her to her feet.

She pulled back to stare at his features. Needing to see him, his eyes and the dear face she'd missed so much. He looked to be in pain, his forehead scrunched while he studied every one of her features. Both her hands rose to caress and lift his hair aside so she could watch him.

He leaned in to kiss her at the side of each eye. "I missed these pretty sparklers. They see more than I feel comfortable revealing. With you, I can't seem to control my feelings."

Cassi stood on tiptoe and returned the favor. "On the other hand, yours are full of secrets."

Next he kissed her nose. "Cute."

She kissed his. "Cuter."

Then he placed his lips on her, his actions bordering on being worshipping. "And, these I missed the most. And their magic."

She loved the way he talked while he kept them joined. She answered. Their breath comingled, adding a layer of sexiness. "The magic only works when we're together."

He lowered his forehead to hers, his eyes never breaking contact. "I swear I'll never leave you again, Cassi, at least, not from choice."

Before she could control it, a sob tore her apart and it broke the spell.

"Don't cry, baby. We're good now. Let me show you." He lifted her into his arms and laid them both onto the bed. Then he rolled on top of her, his arousal huge and throbbing. The pressure from his erection spiked her emotions from weepy to full-on passion.

Both pulled at each other's clothes. She worked his zipper while he undid buttons. In very few seconds, their naked bodies were revealed and entwined.

His mouth devoured her plump breasts as he uttered, "I missed these babies big-time." Caressing their fullness, he slathered each with his tongue, then sucked at the nipples until she cried out from her first orgasm.

Dripping, ready, needy, she angled her hips in such a way as to show him her willingness. Her harsh breathing echoed his as he raised himself over her to enter.

"God, I missed you, darlin'. Never again. Never..." He drove himself into her body and she took him all, blissful and accommodating.

Kissing his cheek, his throat, her hands adoring every bit of skin she could reach, she scraped her nails over the muscles in his back and urged him on.

"You ever leave me again, Trace Maguire and I swear I'll hunt you down and shoot you. Ahh! Yes! Oh, yes..."

He rammed his body into hers, both moving simultaneously, both striving for heaven. The room rang with whispers and groans, whimpers and grunts until with a final hard thrust, he followed her over the edge of sanity and into the realm of incredible, mind-blowing sensation.

Chapter Seven

That night on her way to work, Cassi's heart burst with joy over her earlier interlude with Trace. She clutched his hand tighter and smiled his way. "I could have driven myself, babe."

His chuckle took all censure from his words. "No way! I wouldn't let you do that. I had an ulterior motive. Now I'll have to pick you up after shift and if I behave, I might get to spend the night with you."

"Since when has behaving been a part of your repertoire, detective?" She squeezed his hand to show she teased. "I meant to ask you, Trace, how's your mother? Is Mary Devin working out as her care-giver?"

Trace smiled her way. "Mom is happier than I've seen her in a long time. After we fired the last thieving witch, I'd set up a hidden clock camera in her room but mom keeps telling me to take it down. Guess I'll have to do so when I get around to it. With Mary Devin, I'm certain we won't need it. I want to thank you again for finding her for us."

"I'm so glad. I hope I get to meet your mother soon, while she still feels up to having guests." Trace had told her about the bone cancer and about the pain his mother handled with such grace. He'd even admitted that he wished she'd considered doctor assisted suicide rather than suffering through the next months of unrelenting pain that'll keep getting worse until even the doctors have a difficult time keeping it controlled. The thought of her in such agony had brought tears to his eyes and Cassi'd held him until he'd gained control over his emotions.

"If I could take it away, hell even for one day to give her some relief, I would. I just can't stand to see her hurting."

"I get it, Trace. I do. But this is her choice. Maybe she isn't ready to discuss it yet? Give her time. Let her know you're ready to talk when she is."

"You're right. I've done the research and found the best places we can go to for help. As I told you earlier, when it was first discovered, I e-mailed her the information and added a note saying I'd be willing to make all the arrangements. But I guess it's up to her."

Cassi's heart swelled with pride in Trace's generosity. The man adored his mother so much, he'd willingly put her wellbeing ahead of his own wretchedness. Loving her more than himself, he was prepared to let her go out of his life early rather than keep her around just to suffer longer.

But... not everyone agreed with this philosophy. Seems his Christian mother didn't. And she had the right to make her own choices. What a dilemma?

While her thoughts battled, Trace pulled into the Lipstick Club's parking lot and she noticed the place had been fully repaired after the shootout they'd suffered from weeks before.

She also saw the motorcycles lined up in front and knew that Dani and her boys were already in the joint. The bikes filled her with nostalgia for her brother, Raoul, and she made a mental note to ask Rusty if he'd remembered his promise to find her a bike for her lessons.

Knowing she had to start off riding a motorcycle on one she could handle easier, it was more than time for her to work on her dream of one day using Raoul's Harley.

"Come here." Trace had pulled into the back of the parking lot and was reaching for her.

They kissed and within a few seconds it spiraled to where they couldn't get close enough. Their bodies remembered earlier and needed more.

Cassi wrenched herself from his arms and straightened her clothes. "Trace, behave. You know I need to get inside. We'll have time later, right?"

"Right. Later. Got it." He caressed her cheek and using the same hand behind her head he drew her in for another assault. "I'll be here waiting."

Cutting off their last kiss, she got out of the car and blessed him for making sure the light didn't go on, leaving him unseen by anyone who might be watching. She meandered toward the front door and pulled up when another bike roared into the lot and dangerously cut her off.

Catching her balance, she stopped and waited, not recognizing the person until he lifted the visor and then removed the helmet.

"Fuck, Juan!" She punched his arm and then pushed him. Remembering Trace watching, she calmed down but her voice still rang with disgust. "Bastard, you almost ran me down."

Laughing, Juan held his hands up. "Not a chance. I knew what I was doing, Cass. You were safe, baby. You'll always be safe with me, you know that. I'm your guardian angel."

Hands on her hips, she glared her fury. "Guardian angel? Are you kidding me? Look, you gotta stop messin' with me, Juan. I mean it. No more stalking at night, no more breaking and entering while I'm out, and most of all, no more fucking flowers."

While she'd voiced her demands, his face dropped until she got to the end. Then he completely destroyed her peace of mind. In a hard voice devoid of humor, his eyes without any deceit, he got in her face and growled in a mean voice, "What flowers?"

Chapter Eight

Trace opened the car door, ready to pounce on the asshole who'd scared Cassi. He stopped himself in time. She wouldn't appreciate his interference and he didn't want to make life any more dangerous for her than it already was.

Damn, he wished she'd listen to reason. Her being in that bloody joint made his skin crawl. Filled with misfits, drug users and gang members, in real life, it should be a place that would scare the crap out of her. Instead, she'd made herself fit in.

Hell, he remembered the first time he'd seen her. Flinging herself over her brother's body in the middle of a gun fight, she'd appeared from out of nowhere. If he hadn't rescued her and taken a bullet while doing so, who knew what would have happened.

When they met later, he'd seen a naïve girl with a curtain of black hair to her waist and a rather shy disposition. Hidden inside though was a tenacious spirit, a body that knew every move in a fight and a heart that hadn't yet been awakened. What an oxymoron he'd faced—a nun with the fighting spirit of a warrior and the stubborn inflexibility of an ornery mule.

Whoever killed her twin, Raoul, wouldn't be allowed to get away with it. Her plan to infiltrate the gang responsible—unexplainably her brother's own pals—and find out the names of the three people who'd kicked at his body before they shot him were the ones she meant to hunt down.

Thanks to a confidant she refused to share with him, she'd found out that Tommy Wilkens had been one of the three that night. Armed with that knowledge, she'd set Tommy up to raid the bakery, arranged for Trace and his cops to be there and had gotten the prick arrested. Anticipating he'd be willing to talk to get a lighter sentence, their plan had backfired.

Instead, Wilkens had been killed in prison before they got anything from him. Blasted shame! Oh, not that he'd died. Scum like him, killers with no consciences, they didn't garner any sympathy from him. Still, he regretted not questioning the slimeball before Mendes killed him. If he'd have gotten the other two names, maybe this craziness Cassi refused to let go of, could be put to rest.

Both hands scraped his hair back, and he leaned against the headrest. He knew Tommy had crushed on Dani Andino, the *Armas* gang leader, a woman with no soul. According to Sam, the son of a bitch had been her shadow with the goal of being second in command. Except that a guy called Mani had held that position until the gang shooting a while back at the club had taken his life.

It would have taken Dani's too if Cassi hadn't acted by pulling her out of danger. This fact alone scared the shit outta him because Sam had warned him about Dani's proclivity for women.

La Jefé's attachment to the drugs they sold from the upper floor kept her high and her preferences for females fed her hungers. It wasn't as if Dani hadn't gotten it on with a man whenever the mood struck or it paid off in some way. But when a good-looking chick was around, she lit up. And Cassi was just that.

A classy dame with her new-age look, Cassi's full gorgeous tits and the perfect ass enveloped in a slender form made his mouth water whenever they were in the same room. *Sweet Jesus!* And the way she used those slanted eyes as a weapon to lure a man into her web should be a crime. Problem he had with all of this—that sick boss bitch saw the same beautiful chick he did.

He hoped that Cassi had clued in to Sam's warnings. Telling her would be difficult, yet he had no choice. He'd have to warn her before the wackjob decided to make her move. According to Sam, so far Cassi had kept her at a distance, but

Dani wouldn't be denied for ever. That broad took what she wanted and the hell with the consequences.

Anger boiling over, he threw the car into gear, hit the gas and spun out on the gravel. Straightening the wheel, he drove toward the office where once again, he'd pour over the Santino case. He'd missed something, he knew it. His skin crawled every time he studied those files. So far, whatever obscure clue lurked, it stayed hidden and drove him bat-shit crazy.

Knowing about the *Armas'* illegal activities upstairs at the club didn't help. He'd wanted to go in and arrest the works of them. His asshole of a boss, Chief of Detectives, Hank Lester, had refused his request.

FBI had a sting going on with the Special undercover Agent Sam Smith working the joint. Without that knowledge, Trace wouldn't have been able to drive away and leave the woman he loved behind in that den filled with druggies, sickos and killers.

Chapter Nine

Cass hated the place where she worked. The long, shiny bar at the end of the room shimmered in the gloomy haze of pot smoke and dim lights. The music played low and the room seemed conventional but that wouldn't last.

Soon, the joint would be crawling with either tattooed, bearded bikers or the hoodie-wearing crowd of slackers heading up the cast-iron staircase and returning glassy-eyed and stupid. And she'd have to keep feeding them booze because it was her job—hers and Sam's, her partner behind the bar.

"Hey, sweetheart, you gonna stand there all night watching the fun? Why do I get the feeling you want to run?" Rodrigo Muñoz, the owner of the club, approached and gave her a hug.

"Because I do. When I remember how close we all came to being shot, I have to admit, it was hard to come back."

"Well you can set your mind at ease. We have guards out front now besides in the back. No one will get through to us again, Cass. You're safe."

Sure, like a tiny, stupid bug caught up in a big fat spider web! "Yeah, I know. It's just me being melodramatic." She watched as Dani approached from her special booth. The redhead wore skin-tight jeans with more ripped holes than material. Her bra, visible under the slinky half-top she'd draped over, barely contained her huge breasts. She looked half stoned and all belligerent. "Where have you been, Cass? Sam said you'd hurt your hand. I'm thinking you should give up the boxing bullshit and stick to the job that pays you the most."

Cass bristled and took a deep breath before answering. "Guess you missed me, huh? My hand's good now, thanks." She didn't stick around to see how her snide remarks were taken. Instead, she waved at Sam, made her way to the storage room behind the bar and took down the tight pink shirt with the idiotic lips on the pocket she used as her uniform. When she'd first started here, they'd given her a slinky outfit to wear and she'd refused. Now they didn't hassle her anymore.

She tucked the material into her body-hugging jeans and opened the second button to give the customers a bit of a peek. No way in hell would they get more. She still had some principles after all. Thank goodness, Sam and Rodrigo didn't push it. Squaring her shoulders, she stepped into place and moved close to Sam.

"Hey, Cass, it's good to see you. We're getting busy. I could sure use the help of a pro instead of having to put up with the bozos they had filling in here the last few days."

Before she could answer, a brawl broke out near the slots on the left side of the bar and Cassi moved aside so Sam could intervene. When this type of shit happened near them, Sam tended to get involved rather than wait for the bouncers at the door.

Two bruisers were pounding at each other because one of them had been feeding the slot, gave it up and another stepped in and won. This kind of ruckus happened all the time. These men, more like spoiled little toddlers in a tantrum, couldn't seem to get it that they didn't own any specific machine. When they moved on, it was anyone's bet.

Sam grabbed at the beer-bellied idiot who'd decided the jackpot should be his and pulled him off the winner. Unknown to Sam, beer-belly's buddy took offense and decided to get involved. Skinnier than the others, but fast as spit, he drove his fist into Sam's back.

In seconds, Cass flew over the counter and landed a booted foot in the side of his head forcing him to back off of her bar partner. Angrier than a bobcat with a backside full of buckshot, he turned to her and dove. Bracing herself, Cass nimbly leapt out of his way. Shocked to have missed her, he ended up face first in the bar stools.

Now he was really pissed.

Scrambling to his feet, he tossed aside the stools as if they weighed nothing. Growling his fury, he came at her a second time. And again she sidestepped him. And to make a point, she whipped around to place a kick to the back of his right knee and slow him down. Unfortunately, the idiot couldn't take a hint, it only infuriated him more. Gaining his feet, eyes glittering his intention, he raised his fist and lunged forward.

This time a gun stopped him. The one Dani held to his head. "Make one more move idiot and I swear it'll be your last. You're not welcome in my joint, asshole and you sure as shit don't get to beat up on my bartender. Hell dude, can't you see she's a woman and half your size? Besides, she'd have hurt you. Just be glad I saved you from a hospital visit." Dani grinned at Cass who stepped back, deciding the woman had a point.

"Now take your sorry-lookin' partner and fuck off. Don't come back in my joint again or it'll be the last time anyone sees you walking healthy." She glanced over her shoulder. "Juan, Joey, make sure these guys have gotten the message. But do it outside."

Juan Acedo moved to do her bidding, along with another fellow Cass didn't know other than to see him sometimes with the gang. Juan winked at her before grabbing her opponent and she shrugged off the instinctive revulsion his familiarity caused.

Within minutes, the place was straightened; Sam had recovered and helped her fix the stools. "Thanks, princess. I didn't see the son of a bitch behind me."

"Is your back okay? He hit you pretty hard."

"Yeah, so I'll have a bruise. Won't be the first. I'm just thankful he didn't touch you."

"Hell, Sam. He couldn't catch me." She laughed, her adrenalin taking its sweet time settling down.

Dani stepped forward and put her hand over Cass's where she had it on the bar. When she went to pull hers away, Dani's hand clamped down... hard. Not wanting to cause a scene, somewhat conscious of the gun the girl toted in the back of her jeans, Cass waited with her eyebrow raised questioningly. She didn't see Sam's glower. Dani did.

"What're you staring at, Sam? How about you give us some privacy here, asshole? I want to talk to Cass alone."

"Sure. But if it gets busy, she'll have to kick in. I'm not paid enough to work this bar alone."

Dani's eyes hardened along with her tone. "You're paid to shut the fuck up and do as you're told."

Sam stopped and turned. His eyes were shadowed and Cass couldn't see his thoughts. Her instincts clamored. He wanted to protect her. Before he could react, she spoke. "No problem, Sam. Just whistle if you need me." Cass flipped her hand over to hold Dani's. "So, Dani, what can I do for you?" She led her to the right side where the pool tables were filled with hustlers who paid big bucks to suck in the wannabes. They went to the empty corner table.

Seemingly happy with Cass's change of attitude, Dani's manner became a person with a request not a boss with an order or pulling rank.

From her front pocket, she pulled out her little bottle of disinfectant she carried with her everywhere and squeezed a liberal dose on her hands and held it out for Cass who shook her head. The strong scent of vanilla wafted around them. The switch befuddled Cass big-time and she relaxed.

"Cass, Mani's funeral is happening this Sunday and I need someone to go on behalf of the gang. His mother has made it clear that none of our members are welcome and so I can't go. Neither can Rodrigo because Mani's family'll recognize him. But they don't know you. It's a kind of rule I have that our members get respect from us. So we need a representative."

Shocked, Cass's mind scuttled around to find a reason why this wasn't acceptable to her. "First of all, Dani, I'm not a part of your gang."

"No, you aren't. Yet your brother was. He'd have

understood." Dani stared Cass down. "You know that."

"Yeah, well, I'm not my brother and wouldn't make his choices. And just so *you* know, I never wanted him to join. What he was getting involved in scared me silly."

"Okay, I get it. You aren't one of us. But you work here at the club where Mani hung out all the time. I saw you two cracking jokes together and you always seemed to like him. Couldn't you go as a friend? Take some flowers; I'll pay for 'em... and say some prayers. People like that shit. Turns out, the stupid bastard was religious. Can you just do it for me?"

Cass heard the affection for the guy in Dani's voice and couldn't take offense. It sounded like Dani had cared for him as much as she cared for anyone. Feeling sympathy kick in, Cass nodded. "I can do that, Dani. Not for you. I'll do it because you're right. He was a good guy. Always tipped generously and never gave me a hard time. I liked Mani."

Unhappy with Cass's reply but sensing she'd gotten her way and not to push it, Dani took the funeral notice out of her pocket and passed it on. When Cass went to reach for the paper, Dani grabbed her wrist and pulled her in close. Tenderly, she laid her cheek against Cass's and whispered, "I like a girl who knows her own mind, Cass. Thanks for doing this... for me. Oh, yeah. Happy Birthday, babe." She kissed Cass's cheek, letting her lips linger a fraction too long.

Swiftly, she strutted away and headed to the second floor. Cass picked up the scrunched piece of paper from the table and watched as Dani rudely shoved aside one of the fellows on her way up the stairs.

Chapter Ten

Cass checked the time yet again and sighed with gratitude to see her shift was over. Knowing that Trace would be waiting, she'd hurried through closing up. After redoing her makeup and changing into her own clothes, she called, "I'm off, Sam."

"Hold up, Cass. It was too busy earlier to ask you but I wanted to know what Dani had to say after the fight tonight?"

Cass took the wrinkled paper from her pocket and held it out for Sam. While he read it, she answered. "She wanted me to go to the funeral on behalf of the gang. Said Mani's mother had let it be known she didn't want anyone from the *Armas* members to come. Guess she blames them for getting Mani killed. Dani argued since I wasn't one of the gang, I could go on their behalf and bring flowers. Her respect for him shows she must have some human feelings after all."

"Don't count on it, Cass. The woman's a viper.

Killing to her is as easy as breathing. What did you tell her?"

Cassi still had a bunch of emotions roiling around her upset stomach ever since the interaction with Dani. She didn't know how to share them with Sam so he'd understand her dilemma. "Let's just say, I told her I'd go but for myself and not as a representative for the stupid gang."

He took a step back, his grin faded and his expression became serious. "In those words? You dissed the gang?"

She nodded her head one way, then the other and admitted. "Okay, not in those *exact* words but she got my meaning."

"Gol-darnit, babe, you gotta be careful with that bitch. Promise me. She's got the hots for you, and trust me, you don't want to go there. Ever think it's time for you to back off and quit this joint?" The genuine worry she heard stopped her from taking offense.

Patting his arm, she agreed. "I know you're right and I'll be careful, Sam. Just a little while longer and I might be able to quit as you suggest. I just need a bit more time to find out who killed Raoul."

"So that's why you're here." Sam crossed his arms and his expression hardened. "Honey, you gotta let the cops deal with it. You're so far out of your league, it's ridiculous."

Feeling her back stiffen and her lips tighten,

Cass ignored his advice. And knowing Trace waited, she had no wish to discuss it right then. To appease her friend, she said, "Okay, Sam. I'll give it some thought. See you tomorrow."

Disgust plain, he waved her away. He'd known she'd been stroking him and he didn't like it at all. Hesitating for a few seconds, she gave her head a shake and stepped out into the dark night. Breathing in the clean, albeit hot air cleared her head.

Before she could take another step, bruising arms grabbed her from behind and a rough hand squeezed over her mouth to cut off her screams.

The gun held against her cheek forced her to stop struggling. It was one thing to fight against a physical enemy. Yet completely different when one's opponent had a steel barrel full of bullets digging into her skull. A voice filled with malice whispered harsh words in her ear.

"You and I have some unfinished business to take care of, baby. No one kicks me in the head, makes me look like a fool and gets away with it. No one! Me and my friend here, we figure you owe us some fun for earlier." She struggled. "Uh huh, don't make this any harder than it has to be. Just come with us quiet like, and bitch, if you treat us right, we'll let you live."

Scared, close to soiling herself, she whimpered and prayed that Trace could see what was happening. At the far end of the lot, his car sat in total darkness and there was no movement. Sam's truck was back there too but he was still inside finishing up the night's bank deposit. The two security guys had left earlier, after the joint had closed and locked up for the night. She was on her own and being force-walked to the van they had left open.

Thoughts flashed through her mind like a rock performance video. Used to dealing with instant decisions, she filtered through them and in a flash; one thing became clear. If she let them take her, even if they didn't kill her, she'd wish they had.

Although blood rushed through her veins at warp speed, she had the moves. It was her emotions she needed to control. Shaking, unable to stop her body's reactions, she forced herself to live in the moment and focus.

Knowing she had to scream for help and then hold them off long enough to be heard, she opened her lips until the skin of his hand was between her teeth and bit down as hard as she could. His grunt of pain gave her a huge dose of satisfaction. Once he pulled away, she let loose.

Then using the van for leverage—before her assaulter could shove her inside—she ran up the side of the vehicle, twisting herself out of his hold.

Still screaming like a banshee, she kicked at the waving gun before he could pull the trigger and punched a well-placed jab to the gut of the man moving in on her other side. With nowhere to turn, pinned in by the two furious jerks, she had no option but to dive inside the van and slam the door, catching a hand.

Goodie! That had to hurt, asshole!

With his screams added to hers, she hoped it alerted the others. Scrambling, she whipped around to lock the other back door and then flipped over to the front just as one of them had wrenched the passenger side open. Using her legs as a battering ram, she tried to kick him backwards except his weight stopped her.

Imprisoned by a stinky body, boozy breath and hard hands that had no mercy for soft skin, she strained to reach the horn. Sobbing, screams turning to whimpers, the gear shift digging into her back until the pain was brutal, she reached to gouge her attacker's eyes.

Only it wasn't necessary. A person from outside the car had a hold of his belt and had pulled him to the ground. Trace, his expression furious, repeatedly drove his fist into the other's body. A litany of cuss words followed until she heard Sam yell at him to stop.

Deflating now, strong doses of anger replaced her fear. Exhausted from the earlier adrenalin rush, she slid from the vehicle and slumped to the ground. Realising her shaky legs wouldn't hold her; she could do nothing but watch the show.

Sam had the pot-bellied jerk up against the van, his gun aimed at the fat man's chest. Trace's beating had put the other assailant out cold and he lay in a heap with Trace standing over him, his hair draping his face, hands clenched by his side and his body straining to catch a breath.

"He's done, man. Back off now." Sam's voice soothed, reaching past Trace's fog of fury.

With fists still clenched and trembling, Trace stepped away. Then he whipped around towards her, his face registering remorse and condemnation along with the fading anger.

"Cassi, baby. Are you okay?" He rushed to her side and plucked her from the ground like she weighed less than a flea. Held in his gentle arms, her face hidden against his shoulder, he didn't see her proud tearful smile.

Sam did and this time it was his eyebrow that rose, a question evident in his gaze.

Chapter Eleven

Trace glared at her and the car swerved again. "How many times do I have to tell you that place is a hell hole? It's not safe, Cassidy."

"Yes, you did say that a number of times. And there's nothing wrong with my hearing, Trace, so please, stop yelling at me."

Trace knew his reaction was way over the top but seeing that animal on top of her, forcing her to fight for her life, Trace knew without a doubt, he'd be having nightmares for weeks. And he still hadn't recovered from the last situation where she'd fought off a crazed druggie to save herself and a little girl.

Cassidy Santino had used up his last nerve and he couldn't get through to her. Breathing deep, forcing his voice a few octaves lower, he added, "Baby, you can't know what it does to a man to see his woman handled so brutally and by scum like those two. Sam said you had a run-in with them earlier. Tell me what happened."

With a soothing softness, she spoke and he hated that it worked.

"It was nothing. A slight disagreement."

"Not good enough. Tell me everything." He wouldn't be played by a sweet voice. This was too serious. Every night she worked there, she put her life at risk.

"The fat man took offense at another guy moving in on his slot machine and when it paid off... ahh fatso decided the winnings were his. There was an altercation and Sam moved in to stop the foolishness. Then the sidekick punched Sam in the back and that's when I kinda got involved. No biggie."

Grinding his teeth, impaling her with a look of disgust, he bellowed. "Quit talking like them. *No biggie!* For crissakes, you're a librarian and know how to speak proper English. *Kinda involved...*you kicked the guy in the head and made him look bad in front of his peers. The son of a bitch wanted to pay you back, didn't he? See what revenge can do to people? Turns them into lunatics."

"Hold it, officer. Are you calling me a lunatic? Because some screwball decided he didn't like being made to behave. And in case Sam forgot to add, I didn't stop him. Dani did. With her gun. All I did was defend my co-worker just like he's done for me a number of times."

***

Oh, oh!

Now she'd done it. Trace's face had lost all color. His hands gripped the wheel so hard she feared it might break. "Do tell! And just how many times has Sam had to defend you?"

Sliding back against the passenger door, curling up as a wrongdoing child might, she cleared her throat. "I shouldn't have put it like that. What I meant was, you don't have to worry about me inside the club. There're a lot of people around willing to protect me. And you heard Sam earlier, he's promised to walk me to the car from now on. So I'll be safe in the parking lot also."

"God, I'll never forgive myself for falling asleep. I should have seen what was happening before you had to literally fight for your life."

"Please don't be upset, Trace. You were exhausted. I feel bad enough letting you wait until I get off shift and then having to get up early to go to work. No wonder you dozed off."

"I didn't doze off, I was out cold. Never heard a thing until the screaming started. When I heard your voice, my heart stopped."

"And then you saved me." She caressed his arm. "My hero!"

"Bull! Don't stroke me, Cassi."

"Okay. Let's change the subject now. I don't think I can take much more stress tonight." Hoping by using a different tactic she could sooth his troubled conscience, she reached for his hand.

Thankful when he took hers in his gentle grasp and squeezed, she breathed a sigh of relief. Now she just prayed that Juan, her personal stalker, wasn't outside her house tonight or there'd be hell to pay.

Chapter Twelve

Either Juan wasn't there or he'd found a new hiding place. Relief flared until they entered the house and went into her bedroom. Worn-out, she didn't pick up on the strong scent. Trace's sniffer worked better.

"I can smell pot." He whipped toward her, placed both hands on his hips and waited.

Damn you Juan. After I gave you a warning, you still invade my home? It has to stop.

Her mind scurried in all directions and finding no escape, she broke down and lied. "One of the guys at the... ahh gym gave the marijuana to... ahh Raoul and I found it. I tried it earlier and hated the taste. So I flushed it down the toilet." Not looking his way, she whipped off her blouse hoping to distract him.

It worked until he decided to go into the kitchen and get the room deodorant to spray away the stink.

"Cassi! Can you come here? Now."

The roses! Shit...

She draped a short t-shirt over her naked chest and slipped on some silk shorts to match. Dreading the coming scene, she moved toward where Trace stood with the crushed bouquet of roses on the table in front of him.

He smiled grimly and pointed. "You didn't like them?"

Deciding she'd lied enough for one night, she admitted, "I didn't know who they came from, so no, I didn't like them."

Less hostile now, he asked, "Wasn't there a card?"

She took the card from the drawer she'd thrown it in and could have kicked herself for being too lazy earlier and not putting the damn flowers in the outside trashcan. "Here it is."

He read it and looked at her, his eyebrow raised, his tone reasonable. "Is it your birthday?"

"Yes. Today I'm twenty-nine." *Just answer his questions. No more.*

"And you have no idea who knew about it being your birthday? No one who would send you flowers? A person who would write that they *loved* you?"

"Nope. It's why I didn't keep them."

"What if they'd have come from me?"

"You would have signed the card. And anyway,

it wasn't your vehicle I saw leaving."

Shit!

Like Sherlock Holmes on the trail to solving his mystery, he stiffened. "You were home when they were delivered?"

Oh oh! Cassidy, you're so not good at subterfuge. Whatever you do, don't admit that whoever delivered them broke into your house.

"Ahh... yes. I ran to see who had delivered them after they'd already left."

"Didn't the delivery guy ring the doorbell?" Trace's expression underwent a change and his eyes glittered. Now he was like a Doberman with the scent of meat titillating him.

"Not quite. He just left the flowers." Now she had her hands behind her back like a youngster called into the principal's office.

At this point, Trace lost his cool. "Cassi, what's going on here? Can't you see how irrational this is? Some stranger comes to your door with a huge mass of roses that must have cost a mint, didn't ring the doorbell just left them to die in the hot Vegas weather and drove away. And he wrote I love you on the card." His voice rose with each point he made and by the end, his finger came close to poking her.

Knowing it was his way to react in situations where he sensed she might be in danger, she overlooked his behavior and instead, moved in to wrap her arms around his waist and lay her head against his chest.

He scooped her close and muttered. "Don't think you can sweeten me up like this, Cassi. I want answers."

She felt his warm hand move under her top to stroke her back in his gentle way. "I don't know what to tell you. They arrived out of the blue and I overreacted. After all, if a person cares about me enough to send me this many roses, the least they can do is say who they're from, right?"

He pulled her away so he could see her expression. Since she hadn't yet lied, her innocent act worked. But having him this close, confused and searching, she knew he'd seen through part of her ruse.

"Who sent them, Cassi? You do know."

"Not when they arrived, I didn't. I found out later when Dani Andino, from the Club wished me a happy birthday. I'm pretty sure she sent them on behalf of the gang." *Will he believe her bullshit?*

"Fuck!"

Nope, he didn't believe it for a second. She hid her head against his chest and burrowed in close. "Let it go, Trace. Make love to me and let's forget the rest of the world."

He searched for her lips and kissed her hard. His breathing accelerated, becoming harsh with building passion. She opened her mouth, giving him access and then she melded her body as close to his as possible. Trembling, he picked her up and headed for the bedroom. "Fine, we'll talk tomorrow. Agreed?"

His cell phone rang before she could answer. She'd heard that same ring tone before and groaned. He lowered her to the floor, pulled it from his pocket and held it to his ear. After listening for a few seconds, he muttered a response and ended the call.

"That was Mary Devin. Seems my mom is having a restless night because of some new medications and Mary feels she might settle better if I'm there. I gotta go, baby. I hope you don't mind."

"Of course not, Trace. You have no choice." She kissed him once more and then turned him to face the door. He stopped and turned.

"By the way, I arranged with mom for you to come for dinner Sunday evening. Mary's helping her. They've been like two kids figuring out recipes and happily fussing over every detail. It's keeping them occupied and gives her a special occasion to look forward to so I hope you'll come."

"I wouldn't miss it for the world."

Chapter
Thirteen

Once Trace left, Cass stalked around the house, unable to relax. With her lights off, she went to the window to see if Juan waited in the darkness. Relief coursed through her when she'd decided he was nowhere in sight. Her sixth sense didn't clamor like it did when she was being spied on. The lowlife had her edgy from his relentless lurking.

After locking up tight, she settled in her bed and pulled up the duvet to offset the coolness from the air conditioner. As usual, her thoughts turned to her lover.

The poor guy was being pulled in so many directions; she hated adding to his responsibilities. Some time ago, he'd told her about his boss, Hank Lester, who'd been riding his ass, demanding arrests for the number of recent murders. She knew Trace didn't respect the man or enjoy being on his team, yet that didn't diminish the pressure.

He loved his job and worked damn hard.

Her heart ached for his unhappiness even more when she thought about his mother, Kathleen Maguire, who was withering away with bone cancer. Trace had told her his mom used to be a cop and it was because of her that he'd chosen law enforcement as his career. She couldn't wait to meet the woman he adored. Whenever he mentioned her, his expression showed the love and affection he didn't try to hide. He was a good son and if that was anything to go by, and in her book it was, he'd make a wonderful husband and father.

Tingling at the image her thoughts provoked, she began deep breathing, a technique she used to calm her mind and body; she cuddled into a ball and let her conscience drift wherever it wanted. She wondered how her friend Billy Duran was making out in California in the rehab center she'd paid big bucks for so he could kick his drug habit.

Billy had been around for as long as she could remember. Both her father and brother had helped him break away from his dysfunctional family from as far back as their early teens. They'd all welcomed him into their house when things got rough over at his place. And later, when he'd studied for the bar, he hung out as often as he'd needed sanction.

He'd passed it too. Took top honors. They'd been so proud of him. Working as a defense lawyer, he became quite famous, a man sought after by the wealthy. He'd made a wonderful life, or at least she surmised it had been so. Once his career had taken off, he'd moved to L.A. and they hadn't seen as much of him.

After a few years of being the best, he'd handled a case for a man who'd turned out to be a child rapist. Earning a huge sum of money, paid by the sicko's family, he'd won the trial only for the devil to get released and a short time later get picked up again. This time, the monster had gone too far. The child had died.

Billy hadn't done well knowing his silver tongue and skilled machinations had allowed the animal to go free so he could go out and hurt another innocent.

She'd heard rumors that Billy'd gotten mixed up with a bad crowd and had started on a downhill slide. The last time she'd seen him, he'd landed on her veranda, a mess of a man who'd stopped the street drugs cold turkey and needed help desperately.

Since she'd just found a bundle of money that Raoul had hidden in his locker, and believing it to be dirty drug money, she'd kept it, she used some of it to finance Billy's recovery. Last she'd heard from the facility in California where she'd set up a placement for him; he was doing well.

On her recent call to him, Billy had told her how to deal with Juan Acedo and his stalking. Following Billy's advice, she'd gathered Juan's marijuana butts from the ground, took pictures of where she'd found them in conjunction to her house and had even caught Juan spying from the street on her phone camera as proof that he pursued her some nights.

Her intentions of getting a restraining order had been put on hold only because she didn't want to make any enemies with the gang members. At least, not until she found out for sure who had killed her twin brother.

She knew Juan couldn't be implicated in the murder, which made his bullshit behavior easier to deal with. Rusty himself had told her that Juan hadn't been there at the warehouse the night Raoul had been killed. Instead, he'd been in the hospital, having taken a beating for his refusing to follow Dani's orders to punish Raoul who he'd considered his buddy.

Seems Raoul's initiation had been to kill Sergio Mandalas, the leader of the rival gang, *Los Soldados*. When Raoul had met up with his cohorts, they'd passed on Dani's commands and he'd refused to do such a thing.

What Cassi'd witnessed, hiding behind a fence while spying, was them beating Raoul for disobeying Dani and then shooting him. Cassi still wasn't sure if she'd done the right thing following Raoul that night. If she hadn't of been hiding behind that fence, she'd never have witnessed them killing her twin. Then she wouldn't have this hunger for revenge ruining her life. She might have been able to move on. And not be spending her time with lowlifes like Dani and Juan.

She knew Juan hadn't been at the scene of Raoul's death. However, as a gang member, she had to believe that he'd know who the culprits were.

She could work on him to share the information with her. Maybe if she was nicer, befriended him like she had with Tommy, he might be willing to tell her what had happened.

It was a fact that the guy creeped her out. But now that Dani had let him back into the club, she could work on him there. A shiver ran up her spine and she made a face. The guy was pure yuck! Yet if he could give her answers, she'd do what it took to get them.

The nightmares that plagued her sleep left her in a disgruntled mood the next day.

Chapter Fourteen

Trace hated to leave Cassi's place. He knew she hadn't been straight up about those blasted roses and it annoyed the hell outta him. Aware she'd held back, he'd have drilled her for answers. But the sly little miss had turned his attention to more important matters, like her naked chest. And when she uncovered those beauties, it was all he could do not to drool, drop to his knees and beg to touch. Instantly aroused, no one else could have stroked his fires and changed his mind like that.

Hell, she'd had him so hot for her; he'd hesitated to agree with Mary's request for him to come home. Shame ate away at his conscience. Never before had he found it hard to break away from a woman—whether sex was part of the scenario or not.

Cassidy was altogether different. She'd buried herself so deep into his heart that the thought of life without her would be his interpretation of a living, soul-destructive hell.

Arriving at his mother's house where he had his duplex quarters on the other side of the building they shared, he parked the car in his driveway. Swift as a man with a mission, he cut across the joining sidewalk he'd built from cobblestones and noticed the rooms lit in the back.

He let himself in and made his way to his mother's bedroom at the far end of the house. Wrapped in a fuzzy housecoat, Mary sat with her chair next to the bed, talking low. A small circle of light enclosed the two women.

The moans he heard caught his attention. "Ladies. Thought I'd check in after working late and what do I see? Two old broads having a gossip session instead of sleeping like the rest of the world." He moved into the place Mary vacated and saw the severe suffering his mom couldn't hide.

Her breathing was harsh and the pain lines in her face had deepened. However, as soon as she knew he was there, she'd stopped moaning, no doubt wanting to protect him from her agonizing torment.

"Hi, beautiful. I see you're having a bad night. Mary thinks it's the new drugs?"

"She's right, Trace. Once they kick in, it'll pass. Trust me; I'll be on a high for the rest of the night."

Trace looked over at Mary for confirmation and she shrugged. In other words, she didn't know if the drugs were working as well as they should have been.

"Never mind me, boyo, what the hell are you doing out so late? Trace, my lad, you need your sleep too. I've seen you looking haggard as hell for the last while. I know it's that bloody case you're working on, Cassidy Santino's brother's murder." For a few seconds, she stopped talking and caught her breath. Biting her lip, she waited it out and then relaxed.

"Hey, are you spying on me old woman?"

"Cut out the old woman crap and no, for your information, I don't have the energy to spy on a grown man who should know better."

"Right! So you've gotten Mary to do it."

"Of course." She grinned, a little of her old cheekiness lighting the beloved face of a woman who'd endured unrelenting torture and saw no end soon.

"Can you take a little whiskey with this medication?" He'd used this trick before to give her relief. The doctors would shit if they knew but the worst thing that could happen is it would kill her. And, at this point in her illness, they both knew that would be a blessing.

In the earlier days, he'd begged her to let him take her overseas to one of the European countries whose laws allowed doctors to assist in one's passing. She'd refused, said she didn't believe they should mess with the Almighty's plan.

Mary left the room and returned with the expensive bottle of Irish whisky both he and Kathleen preferred and a tray holding three glasses. By the time she'd filled them all, and passed him his, the patient had slipped into medicated oblivion and knew no pain for the moment.

Tiptoeing, he and Mary moved into the living room. She carried the baby monitor in case Kathleen needed her. He dumped the tray on the coffee table, passed out their drinks and then slumped on one of the two easy chairs.

Mary started the conversation. "She's worse."

"I know. The pain must be excruciating."

"It is. The medication gives her relief but it's temporary. Tonight, I upped the dosage so she could get some sleep. The doctor's coming in the morning and I'll get him to prescribe a different dosage. This amount isn't working as well as it should. Each patient is different. Some have a surprising low pain tolerance. Your mom's is so high that it's hard for us to regulate."

"She's a fighter."

"True. We both know the end will still be the same. She told me earlier she was sorry now that she hadn't let you make the arrangements to take her overseas."

He bolted forward. "She said that?"

"Yes. Sadly, it's too late for that now. She couldn't handle the trip, it would be absolute torture."

Deflated, he took a big gulp and slammed his glass into his free hand. "Will she be up for the dinner on Sunday? It's only two days away but I don't want her to be overtaxed."

"Oh, yes. You must let her have her party, Trace. It's all she's talked about for days. Meeting your young lady and vetting her. I swear she's like a four-star General in the U.S. army. Just so you know; your Cassidy is in for a real inquisition from Kathleen. She keeps telling me all the questions she means to ask and then changes her mind. It's what's kept her happy, so please make sure it happens."

"Cassi's already agreed to come. We'll make it a night for Mom to remember." He stood to leave and almost turned back when he heard whispering behind him.

Had sweet old Mary actually said what he thought she had?

"Her last night..."

Chapter Fifteen

Next afternoon, Cassi showed up at the gym in time to pacify Rusty about her being at the fight that night. "Sure, I'll be there—got Sam to cover the beginning of my shift so I can help you with Arlene at the club."

"Good. That girl gets so rattled before a fight, it's all I can do not to punch her myself. The last few bouts out of town were nerve-wracking to say the least. Glad tonight we're back home in Vegas so you can be there. You seem to have the knack of keeping her calm."

"Glad to help, you know that, love. Sorry I wasn't able to travel." Changing the subject, Cass checked over the schedule she'd helped Rusty set up for Arlene's practice sessions. Turns out, the girl had some major matches lined up and would need to stay focused on her training.

"Wow, Rusty, you've worked hard to get this girl

all the good fights. She'll be competing with some of the best out there."

"Yeah! I know. The brat's good enough. If only she didn't think she was infallible. Won't listen to our advice half the time and the other, she's just plain mean."

"Mean can work for you in the ring. You know that."

"Sure. It's crucial for some fighters. But that girl's got a kind of darkness buried deep in her soul. I shoulda kicked her ass outta here when she first came to the gym sniffing around and I didn't. There's something about the dame that gets to me. She reminds me of someone." Rusty scratched at his hair through the black tuke he never took off.

Cassi paid attention. She'd thought the same thing herself and had pushed the notion away as being fanciful. "Do you know who?"

"Nah! The broad moves a lot like you. She's imitating and that tells me she's sharp. She has a way of twisting her head that gets to me. Hell, I don't know why it should. The thing is, she's good. Has stamina and strength. Wants to win and that's half the battle. Just wish she had more heart for the sport. "

"Well, my friend. You can't have it all. Could be once she wins more bouts, you'll see the love shine through."

"Fat chance in hell. All I see is a broad who'll want a bigger cut of the purse."

"You cynical old man, you! Stop pretending you don't care." Cassi one-arm hugged him and laughed when he bristled. Then she choked up when he caressed her cheek, his aged hand tender.

"You're my dream fighter, Cassidy Santino. The skills, the moves, more heart than most – everything but the need to win. Monkey, you could give this old man a thrill like none other." His heavy sigh arrowed straight to her heart. "Guess it's not meant to be." When he stood, his bones cracked in his knees and the grimace he couldn't hide caught her attention. Rusty was getting on in age. He had to be in his late sixties. The thought of life without him was fleeting and painful. She needed to spend more time with her old friend outside of the gym.

Before she could voice her idea of them having dinner together soon, Arlene knocked and entered.

Dark hair pulled back in a tail, her brown eyes suspicious, she glanced from one to the other and a sneer appeared. More muscular than Cass, yet the same body shape, her armor in place, she asked, "You guys gonna sit on your asses all day or do we have a practice planned. You realize that Sara Flight is my opponent tonight and we all know, she's a fucking robot, fast and furious." Arlene sneered at the other girl's tag line her team had been using for promotion.

"Yeah, yeah! We're coming, just organizing your

next few fights. We want you should have a chance to challenge a championship bout – maybe next year."

"Hell, old man. I'm not waiting around that long. You get me as many fights as you can. The more I win, the faster I can get into the ring with a known fighter who counts. I need to make some big money soon."

"Hey, don't you go telling me what I need to do, Arlene. I'm the boss and don't you forget it. Now you two get into the ring and work on your punches. This Sara chick is dynamite with her uppercuts."

As the two girls walked toward the smaller ring, Cassi felt the other recoiling as usual. Suddenly, it was all too much. This weird female had been consistent in treating Cass shabbily. And for no reason that Cass could figure out. Jealousy, the excuse she'd used for Arlene's behavior from the first time she'd met her, had always been the answer. But hell, when was the stupid girl gonna let go of such pettiness?

Her heart heavy from having to face the petty spitefulness every day, she spit it out. "Arlene, you ever gonna tell me what the hell I did to you to make you hate me so much?"

Arlene stopped dead and swiveled to glare Cassi's way. Her brown eyes deep, hiding emotions that her words betrayed. "Hate you? Fuck Cass. I don't care enough to hate you. All you are to me is my sparring partner. You're here to help me be a better fighter. So let's just get it done, girl."

Spouting off, Arlene grabbed her mask and gloves and turned toward one of the workers to help her get outfitted. Then, impatience obvious, she waited while the same employee took care of Cass.

Once in the ring, Rusty approached and gave them the order to start. From then on his voice rang out with either foul language or praise. All aimed towards his fighter.

Chapter Sixteen

Sore from the workout Arlene had delivered, knowing she'd taken a lot more punishment than she'd needed to, Cassi hoped the boost in morale would carry Arlene through her pending fight in a short while.

As tough as Arlene acted, every once in a while Cass saw through the other's bullshit and the scared, unhappy soul lurking behind the armor appeared. This person tugged at Cassi, the sad girl who covered her fear with fake bravado and downright orneriness.

As tough as she tried to be, when Cassi measured her against Dani Andino, the leader of the *Armas* gang, there was no comparison. Dani was the real deal, as heartless as they come, soulless and narcissistic. She scared the crap out of Cass. Damned if she didn't scare the hell out of everyone who knew her.

Later, helping Rusty in the change room, Cassi watched as Arlene prepared for the coming match. Her outfit, red silk top and matching shorts, fit her well, giving her the professional look Rusty demanded. *Rusty's Gym* embroidered on the back of her shirt drew the eye like it was meant to.

Totally focused, she still appeared antsy, ready to battle anyone who spoke out of turn.

"Calm down, Arlene. Considering this is the first fight of the night, there's a big crowd out there and they've come to see you. Word's getting out that you're a skilled boxer on her way up."

"You think, Rusty? I do give them a good show, right?"

"Yeah! Now tonight, I want you to make it last longer. Don't go for the knockout too early. Play with her a little; let them see your moves."

Cassi nodded in agreement. "The judges like being made to keep score. It's how they assess the fighter. If they like you, their evaluation will add to your worth. Then you'll have more boxers wanting to go up against you, right?"

Arlene stared at Cass as she listened. Her whole being seemed to be concentrating on the words and all the time she nodded. "Yeah. I get it. I gotta lead her on; let my points build up. Then I'll punch the bitch into tomorrow."

Cassi laughed, couldn't help it. Ignoring Rusty's disgusted shaking of his head; she grabbed Arlene's shoulders and shook them with affection.

"Right!"

Soon they had made their way to ringside and saw the attendants were seating the audience and the large auditorium had been set up for the match with the lighting and judge's area ready to go.

The lingering scent of other matches permeated the air and took Cass back to when her father had allowed her to come and visit him before some of his matches.

Once Arlene had settled into her corner and Cassi and Rusty prepared her equipment, the referee called for order and the two fighters were introduced. Although Sara got a good round of applause, Arlene's was louder and few of her fans stood and made a huge fuss. Though Arlene put on a show by holding her hands up in the air and dancing around the ring, she played it low key and soon the crowd had taken their seats and the fight began.

In the first round, Sara outboxed the less experienced Arlene. She knew what looked good and used all her tricks. Not happy with the treatment, Arlene plunked back into her seat, spit out her teeth guard and glared at Rusty. "You wanna tell me what the hell I'm doing out there, playing with this fool. I could have knocked her out twice already."

"Jesus, girl, don't let her get away with that shit. We didn't tell you to stop fighting, just don't go in for the big hit for a few rounds. Now, get your ass back in there and box her."

Cassi added, "Start raking up points, Arlene. You know how. Just like we practiced today. Draw her in, use your footwork to throw her off her stride. Play with her, girl. Like I do with you."

"What?" Arlene's eyes shot fire at Cass. Radiating aggression, she leaned toward her just as the bell rang. Rusty shoved her guard at her face and she opened her mouth but her eyes glared a message. *Bitch!*

Into stride, pissed from Cass's comment, Arlene began using techniques she'd learned in the ring from sparring. Her footwork kept her moving and out of range of a lot of Sara's clinching intentions. She placed her punches well, following them with a right jab, a left cross punch and then a right uppercut.

By the end of round three, Sara had upped her game and came in with intentions of finishing off the match. By then, Arlene had her number and a well-placed knockout punch hit the other squarely on the chin and down she went.

Jumping, pumped from the excitement, Arlene raced to ringside and hit the ropes hard, over and over, until Rusty grabbed her shoulders and turned her to him. Before anyone knew she would, Arlene gave him a huge hug and then high-fived Cass.

Calmer after seeing Rusty, she went over to accept her win and Cass looked over the crowd. These diehards could sniff a winner from out of hundreds. No doubt, they'd paid attention tonight and would be taking note of Arlene's name.

One face stood out from all the others. Trace nodded and left her tingling from the power of his raised eyebrow and self-conscious grin. Seems the guy had trouble staying away from her.

She waved his way. Then she answered Rusty's question. When she looked back, he was nowhere in sight.

Chapter Seventeen

Still high from Arlene's win and Trace's smile, Cassi entered the Lipstick Club and gave a silent thanks for it being rather empty for a Saturday night. Mind you, it wasn't yet ten o'clock, and for Vegas, that was like the middle of the day.

Once ready, she slipped behind the bar and grinned at Sam who was deep in a discussion with a snazzy lady who looked out of her element.

Scanning the room, she made her way to some of the tables that needed clearing. *Where is everyone tonight?* She emptied a few of the booths and headed for the side area where they had the pool tables.

One of the new girls they called Toby was schmoozing with a few of the boys in the far corner and Cass waited to catch her eye. Toby made her way over, her expression puzzled. "You want me, Cass?"

"Where's everyone tonight?"

"Don't know. It's been kinda quiet. Floss went upstairs a while back and never came down. I told her to stay out of that place. I think one of the guys told her they had some good shit up there and she felt in the mood for a hit."

Understanding the language after working in the joint for so long, Cass asked, "Which room did she go through?"

"You're kidding, right? You mean to tell me you've never been up there?"

"Nah! I'm not into that crap, I'll stick with booze. Sam's warned me to keep away from the upstairs so – no – I haven't been there."

"Fuck, Cass, you're like a friggin virgin around here then. We've all had a taste of Dani's product. It's damn good. Look I'll cover for you if you want to go and say hi to the guys. You know them all; they're always at the bar."

"You think I should? I've been curious about the second floor ever since I started working here."

"Hell, sure I'm sure. The first room is Dani's office. Then they have the lounge where the young girls all hang out when they're not working in the smaller alcoves. The other big room is locked up tight. I figure they count a lot of money in there because they have armed guards posted every minute."

Ignoring the last part of Toby's message, Cass's heart dropped. "You say young girls? How young?"

Toby stilled. Her gaze raked over Cass's face and then she relaxed. "You knew there were girls working those rooms, right? I mean I didn't tell any secrets."

Cass nodded, keeping the revulsion from showing in her expression. "Sure I knew. I guess I figured they were experienced prostitutes not under-aged kids."

"Trust me, Cass them whores are as experienced as they need to be. Rodrigo watches over them like a hawk and Dani's favorite is looked after real well."

Cass hid behind the curtain of her hair. Her hands went into her back pockets of her jeans and she licked her lips to play for time. As shocking as this all was, she didn't want Toby to stop sharing. She needed to chill.

"Okay, can you cover for me for a few minutes? I'll just go up and take a peek. Fucking curiosity is going to get me into trouble one day. I know I should be smarter, but.... I ain't."

Toby giggled just as Cass hoped she would. "Sure, I'll tell Sam you're in the ladies room if he asks. Go have some fun."

Cass went up the stairs, hesitating at the top and looked along the railing. From there, she saw a long passage with three innocuous doors overlooking the bar. Knowing she never saw anyone use those doors except for the first one where Rodrigo hung out, she continued further down the hallway and rounded the first corner.

There, she saw the business of the upstairs. Music came from further down and she stopped at the open doorway to see three girls, all who looked buzzed, working the men in the room.

Two couples were dancing a slow waltz. Their bodies glued while their hands traveled everywhere. A drunk was slouched in a big easy chair, while a semi-naked dancer performed a lap dance. Another girl, a young blonde with straggly hair hanging to her waist, was backed against the wall, her expression vacant and uncaring. Totally absorbed, a big fellow had her pinned with his undulating body while her half-covered breasts obviously had his full attention.

Then she saw Floss in the corner, struggling to get away from an overzealous idiot who'd decided she was his choice for some evening's entertainment. Figuring the girl could handle herself, Cass checked out the rest of the large room.

There was a bar covered with half-full glasses, empty beer cans tipped over and white powder spread out with various sniffing apparatus. Spills on the floor and the stench of sex, booze and drugs had Cass turning away in disgust.

Until she heard the sound of flesh hitting flesh and realized that Floss's playmate wasn't playing. The creep had no intention of being denied. Stepping closer, she heard Floss yell. "I'm not one of the girls up here. I'm just a waitress downstairs. Leave me alone."

"Fuck, do I look like I give a damn? You'll do me just fine. In fact, I like a little spirit in my fillies."

Struggling for real now, Floss yanked away from his groping hands only to have her shirt ripped open and her large breasts appear which tempted the idiot even more. He reached again, his hands gripping, pinching... hurting. "Get away from me you stupid perv." Panic ripped through her voice and Cass had had enough.

Reaching from behind the guy, she wrenched his belt which forced him to step back. As soon as he did, she grabbed his thumb, twisted hard and kicked out his right knee. In total control, she leaned toward his head and whispered, "You move and I'll break it. Nod if you understand."

He nodded and Cass caught Floss's eye and gestured her toward the door, telling her without words to escape while she had the chance.

Once Floss had left and Cass knew the others in the room hadn't even noticed the ruckus in their corner, she gave one last jerk on his thumb and said. "I suggest you leave. But if you want to make a scene, I'm your girl."

"The boys told me I'd have a good time here. That's a bunch of bullshit. I'm gone."

"Good decision."

Rising to his feet, cradling his right hand in his left, he stomped past her to the back of the room and disappeared.

Making sure he didn't change his mind, Cass watched until he left. Then with her mind on what just happened, she didn't pay attention to where she was heading and turned the opposite way. Some instinct stopped her in the open doorway of the next room and what she saw made her blood run cold.

Horrified, backing away, she collided with the person who'd come up behind her. Finding her arms being gripped by Dani and the other's eyes digging holes in her shield, she stepped back only to have Dani move along with her. Their bodies were close together, closer than Cassi felt comfortable with. Her personal space didn't allow just anyone to invade. Trace had full rights to it.

Rather than make excuses for her being there, Cass waited. She willed herself not to let her revulsion and angst show. After all, from what she could make out, the hoard of drugs shocked her silly. Yet the stacks of money, all illegally attained, would keep the entire population of the city's poor fed for a week. *My God, aren't there laws against this shit?*

"You looking for me, Cass?"

Now what could she say? If she said yes, she'd have to come up with a reason. If she said no, then why was she there? Something told her only the truth would pass muster with the savvy bitch who wouldn't back off.

"Nope. I've worked here for a while now and never did get upstairs. Guess my feminine curiosity got the better of me."

"Hey, girl, you know what that did to the cat—got it killed." Dani's warning didn't go unheard.

Playing the game, Cass answered with a grin. "So, you gonna kill me for being a female?"

Dani raised her hand and brushed Cass's hair back behind her ears. "Why do you hide behind your hair all the time, darlin'? You got secrets?"

Cass willed herself not to move. "Doesn't everyone? Bet you got more than most, Dani."

"Oh sugar, I got some secrets that would turn your hair blue for real not just from the spray shit you use." Dani's fingers caressed the curtain of softness that Cass had sprayed with a shimmering of blue while getting ready for the job.

Then she jiggled the large earring dangling from the opposite side where Cass's head had been shaved and tugged at it playful like. "You're the only chick I know who wears a different earring in both her ears. I like it."

All of a sudden, she seemed to remember where they were and straightened, drawing Cass by her hand into the hallway. Before she closed the door, she yelled. "Where's Randy or Ken? One of them should be guarding this door every fucking second. How many times I gotta tell you."

Ken, one of the regulars Cass knew from the

bar below, stepped forward. "I'm here, just helping Mike open this crate."

Dani approached the guy and backhanded him so hard, his head jerked sideways. Though his expression hardened, he took it. "You're paid to guard. I don't pay you to be a nice guy. No more chances, Ken. Got it?"

"Yeah, boss. Sorry." He scurried past Cass and stopped in the hallway, standing sentinel outside the now closed door.

Cass started to wander back downstairs, hoping she'd gotten away with her foolishness.

It wasn't to be. Dani grabbed her arm and pulled.

She shouldn't have...

Chapter Eighteen

Pure reaction took over and Cass's reflexes kicked in. She swiveled, using her back and Dani's hand to flip the shocked deva up and over. At the last minute, she pulled back from landing the follow-up punch to the solar plexus that ended the action and instead, she made sure the other landed softly, without getting hurt.

When Dani twisted from under her and flipped her off, she let her. And when Dani—eyes blazing astonished glee–pushed her away so she landed on the floor near the wall, she allowed herself to be manipulated.

That's when she felt the gun in the side of her head and Ken's growled warning. "Stop now, Cass. Stay down."

Obeying his instructions, her heart beating harder than her breath could deal with, she wanted to drop her head to the floor and just lay there.

Instead, she scuttled backwards.

Dani laughed and held out her hand. Cass breathed a silent prayer of thanks, extended her own and let the other draw her to her feet. "Ken, get that gun away from her, man. Can't you see she was just showing off her moves? This girl don't like being touched and I forgot that."

"I'm sorry, Dani." Again, truth seemed more likely to be accepted than bullshit and so Cass admitted. "I was a bit spooked and reacted without thinking. I'll go back downstairs where I belong. I shouldn't have come uninvited."

Dani's expression lightened. "Yeah, well you have my invitation to come up here anytime you want... to see *me*." Steel flooded her eyes and her mouth formed a tight line only a fool would ignore. "Otherwise, stay the hell away from this part of the joint."

Not moving, Cass let the words echo in the silence. She tilted her head so the curtain of hair slid away and let a small smile fill her face. "Thanks, Dani."

Cass headed downstairs and saw Sam's face. Furious would be an understatement. By the time she'd made her way around behind the counter, he had it under control. Despite his nonchalance, she had no doubt, she'd be hearing from him as soon as time permitted.

Sure enough, he hit on her about fifteen minutes later. First he stared into her eyes and his seemed to relax once he saw for himself that they were normal. "What the fuck, Cassi? Are you crazy girl? I told you upstairs was out of bounds."

"I know, Sam. I'm sorry, okay? Toby and I were talking and curiosity took over."

"You mean nosiness. Look princess, the shit that goes on up there isn't anything you need to worry about. You work the bar. Nothing more, nothing less. If you won't keep your head straight and do your job then you're fired. Can't put it plainer than that, now can I?"

Bristling, still full of adrenalin from her dangerous encounter with Dani, she came back at him. "You can't fire me. Rodrigo was the one who hired me."

Eyes narrowing, Sam's face hardened. "You wanna push it?"

Realizing she was acting like a brat, that her harrowing experience upstairs was making her stupid, she relaxed and pushed her hair back so he could see her face. "I'm sorry, man. I'm being an ass. And you're right. Of course, you are. I shouldn't have been up there. What I saw can't be unseen and now I'll have more nightmares to deal with."

Gauging her sincerity, Sam also reacted. "Goddammit, Cassi. Do you know how I felt when I saw you and that vicious she-cat come out of the hallway together? And then you flip her over like she's no one special. Shit, I'm not sure I could have made that shot from here to stop Ken from shooting your ass. Dude, don't ever do that to me again. Promise me."

Shocked to the core from hearing his words, Cass moved next to him and bumped the side of her body against his. "You would do that for me?"

Realizing what he'd said, Sam seemed to gather his thoughts and bumping her back, he grinned. "Hell, with my aim, I'd've probably shot you. Go serve your customers and quit being a pest." He tugged her hair and went back to work.

Laughing, Cass checked the end of the counter and noticed Juan's impatience. As she approached, she saw him scratch at the mass of hair on his arm and a fleeting thought couldn't be dismissed. With all that body fuzz, the man looked part werewolf.

"You and Sam seem to be pretty friendly."

"He's my boss and a good friend. Like you, Juan. I need all the friends I can get."

Slipping into her new role of buddy to her stalker, she wiped the counter and asked, "What's your poison?"

"A shot of tequila and a Bud Light."

"Coming right up. It's quiet in the joint tonight, ain't it?"

"Yeah. Dani has most of the guys working the warehouse."

She raised her eyebrow and didn't comment. It worked.

"Let's just say, they have a big shipment needs to

be distributed."

Cass got the feeling that Juan was showing off and she played along. "And you're not there because...?"

"She still has to protect the club. I'm guarding outside again until they shut down. Even though the bar closes at 2am, sometimes we're still open upstairs for hours after."

Cass looked around to make sure they weren't overheard. "Do you guard the back? It must be pretty busy sometimes?"

"Sure is. Some nights we get as many customers as you guys have in the bar. We're just not open to the public. You don't have an invitation from Dani or Rodrigo, or you're not a gang member, then you don't get in."

Cass had to keep him talking. "So, the *Armas*... they treat their members well?"

"Sure. That's why a lot of us dudes joined with them when they started the club. Dani knows how to treat us boys right."

"Except for my brother, they shot him." The words broke free before she could haul them back and to cover up, she added. "The idiot never did know how to follow orders." Heart breaking for disrespecting her hero, Cass shook her hair forward so Juan couldn't read her guilt.

Juan's face fell and he dropped eye contact. Instead, he gulped his shot of tequila and then guzzled from his can of beer.

Knowing she'd gone too far, Cass changed the subject. "Detective Maguire is sure pleased with Mary's care for his mom. He's invited me to visit his mother tomorrow night, so I'll say hi to Mary if you like." Playing the hunch that Juan would have learned about her visit from Mary, his step-mom, it paid off.

"I know. She told me. Guess you've been lying about him just working your brother's case. My mom says he's your boyfriend." Voice deepening with accusation, Juan stiffened.

Cass stood straight and glared. "My boyfriend? I don't have boyfriends, dude. I'm my own girl. Who I choose as friends and see once in a while is my business. No one owns me." She hoped she'd played this right. How much longer would he believe her story about Trace and her not being involved? Time for her to come clean and put it into perspective.

"I guess." His weird eyes searched hers and she held his look for as long as she could, glad when he slumped and drained his beer. She got him another. "This one's on me, hon."

He lifted it towards her as a salute and took a drink. "I heard you were asking questions about the night your brother got shot."

Floored, not sure how his mind worked or why that subject came up, she nodded and waited.

"Everyone was talking about you tackling Dani about it."

"Ahh... yeah, well let's just say I stepped outta line. But I had to ask. You know? He was my brother."

"I'm really sorry about that night, I was—"

One of the fellows stepped up behind Juan and slapped him on the back. "Can I get one of those?" He pointed at the beer can and waited.

Shit!

Chapter Nineteen

Trace couldn't stop thinking about Cassi. The little darling invaded his thoughts all the time, moments when he least expected it. Quite often, he found himself grinning like an idiot and hiding an uncomfortable bulge in an embarrassing area.

Earlier, he'd gotten home after putting in some grueling hours on a new case where a father had absconded with his two children and had left the mother locked in the basement of their home only for her to dig out his old army gun and shoot herself.

Seems she'd been bonkers for the last few years and the dad had fretted about her care of the kids. Why she'd killed herself, no one knew? The husband had left her phone with her so she could call a friend to come and let her loose. Except, she hadn't chosen that way to help herself. Poor family... Guess the sucker had been right to worry.

After a quick trip next door to check on his mom only to find her sleeping for once, Trace headed to his own place for a shower, to change out of his working garb and into his comfortable jeans and a regular shirt that didn't need a stinking tie.

Settling in front of his new smart TV with a cold beer, he let his thoughts flow and they headed straight for the gorgeous, blue-eyed babe who'd become a permanent resident in his head.

Suddenly, the schedule on her fridge came to mind and he remembered Rusty's had a match that night at City Center. Knowing she'd be there, he surged to his feet and headed for the driveway and his vehicle.

If he hurried, he'd be in time to watch from the sidelines. No doubt, Rusty and Cassi would be there putting their girl through the paces and taking care of her needs.

Sure enough, the crowd had gathered and the fight had just begun. Arlene looked to be holding back. The other fighter barraged her with hits which she either countered or dodged. Something didn't look right.

At the end of round one, she headed back to her corner and looked to be in a tizzy until Rusty had a serious talk with her and even Cassi put in a few words. After that, the whole vibe changed. Now Arlene began fighting with earnest. She made a lot of points that he could see and the judges were paying close attention.

She followed up another round with the same kind of display only to annihilate the other fighter at the end with a knockout punch that left her on the floor while the referee counted her out.

He wasn't much of a boxing fan. Yet this match had been entertaining and he picked up on the crowd's enthusiasm.

To make the night special, as soon as she saw him, Cassi sent him a grin that made his stupid heart flutter like it had as a teenager getting his first feel. He wanted to rush over and snatch her into his arms. *Jesus man, you're in deep this time. This girl smiles and your insides turn to goop.*

He watched as the three joined in the celebration hugs given to a fighter who'd done her job well. That Arlene won didn't surprise him, she had the moves. What shocked the shit out of him was knowing that Cassi could have beaten both those women with very little effort. A premonition came over him and the now empty, innocent ring took on a sinister kind of aspect.

He didn't like the dark place his mind had gone or the sense that he'd soon find out if his hunch was right.

Blasted hell! He needed to see her... tonight. And he couldn't wait until after she finished work. He'd grab a bite and then head over to the club. Unknown to her, it was a new habit he'd gotten into lately.

Chapter
Twenty

Cassi didn't notice Trace enter the joint, she never did. He'd followed another customer in and sat in an empty booth in the back of the room.

His navy hoody, ripped jeans and black skater shoes helped him fade into the dark area and his ball cap pulled low over his eyes to shade his features worked to keep him incognito while he nursed a beer.

Therefore, she had no way of knowing he'd seen her come downstairs after the interaction that had taken place.

When she'd cozied up to Juan, he must have watched her every move but still didn't make himself known. It wasn't until one of the girls commented on the hunk in the corner that she even had an inkling her man was there at all. Once she became aware, her skin tingled with pleasure. Taking a cold can of Coors, his favorite; she shimmied over to his seat and sat across the table from him.

He lifted his face and that's when she saw the look in his eyes.

Oh, oh! She'd never felt afraid of the man before. Now a frisson of fear travelled along her backbone and dumped into her stomach making it clench and her swallow hard.

"Don't be mad, Trace."

"You were upstairs."

"For a few minutes. I was curious."

"Why did the girl run down with her blouse torn?"

"Some guy got frisky. He left."

His eyes narrowed and he stared at her discomfort. "What did you do to make him leave?"

"Just a little suggestion. He wanted to go, I didn't make him..."

"Bullshit."

"I might have convinced him this wasn't the funhouse he expected. Really, Sam was watching my back."

"No, Sam was downstairs. You were upstairs. All he did was watch in horror while you flipped the boss."

"Trace, Dani didn't take it personal. She..."

"She wants you. That's why she didn't."

"I saved her life."

"She wants you. And what Dani Andino, bitch boss wants, she takes." His eyes drilled his message's impact into the silence as much as the harsh way he'd spoken the words. "Am I getting through to you, Santino? That bitch only cares about drugs, money and herself. You don't matter even a smidge. She's playing you because she wants to screw you."

"Why are you being like this, Trace? I know you're worried about me. You don't have to be. I'm handling things."

His manner still cold, he changed the subject. "What did the furball want? You were all pally with him."

"You mean, Juan?" Knowing she had to calm Trace if possible, she grinned weakly and admitted, "He's a bit of a sleaze but he knows who was at the warehouse the night my brother was killed. I almost had him talking about Raoul and then we were interrupted. One thing he did say that you might not know. The reason the bar is so empty tonight is because most of the gang are working at their warehouse. He let it out that a big shipment has arrived."

Now she did have his attention. He stiffened and asked, "Did Sam hear about this?"

"No, I don't think so. Why?"

He pulled out his phone and his fingers flew over the keys as he formatted a text message. Then he stood to leave. "Sorry, Darlin', gotta go. Can I come over later?"

She got to her feet, flipped back her hair and

gave him the full treatment including a flirty suggestive look. "Will you keep giving me a hard time?"

Softening, his eyes shot her a promise. "Oh baby, I have full intentions of doing just that." With a quick squeeze of her waist, he went past her and headed for the door. With every step he took, her eyes followed hungrily. That man's sexy way of walking made her lust-filled eyes cross. With personal knowledge, she knew his moves could drive her over the edge and had done so more than once.

Chapter Twenty-one

Still feeling the effects of Trace's visit, Cass decided it was time to use the phone number she'd memorized after the night Sergio Mandalas, leader of the rival gang, Los Soldados, had stopped by her house and scared the dickens out of her.

Thankful that he hadn't been there to hurt her, instead he'd come to tell her he'd found out the reason Raoul had been shot. Her brother had refused to carry out the hit Dani had put on Sergio. And because they'd hung out a few times in the past, Ray had even warned him about the planned assassination.

So, now Sergio felt an obligation to Cassi and had left his personal cell number with her to be used if she needed his help. Payback was a bitch according to Sergio but he had a conscience. She knew that.

Heading for the washroom, she pulled her cell

phone out of her pocket and carried it along. Then she made sure the room was empty before placing her call.

"Yeah!"

"Hi, Sergio. It's me. Cassidy Santino."

"Yeah, I saw the number. What's up?"

His terse reply grated. Two could play at this game. Cutting to the chase, she asked, "Did you find out any more information about Raoul's murder?"

"I told you I'd get back to you."

"You didn't."

"Cause all I know is who was there, not the shooter."

Her heart began pounding, almost to the point where it deafened her from the surrounding sounds. Clutching the phone now slippery from her sweating palm, she felt the tears gather. "Tell me now."

"Look, Cass. Let me take care of this. I can handle it better than you, it's what I do."

"Sergio, I need to know." Her voice sounded cold even to her.

"Okay! So... Miguel was killed at the scene, right? The other guys were Tommy Wilkens and some dude called Acedo. And, Cass there's a lot of talk about a chick being involved also. Just don't know who."

A flood of fury consumed her. The overwhelming emotion turned her into a statue.

She couldn't speak or move and his next words made no sense. "What?"

"I said; don't do anything until I find out the rest. Then I'll take care of that bastard Acedo and we'll get that bitch Dani while we're at it."

Words burst out. "You think it's her?"

"Hey, all's I know is mouths are closed tight on this one. It cost me big to get even that much out of the boys. Gotta tell you, it took some persuasion – in a physical sense if you know what I mean. So listen honey, don't go spooking anyone so they catch on that we're close."

His words rattled around until they made sense and she went to speak when she heard another voice on his end calling to him. "Sergio, we're ready to hit the warehouse now. The crew is waiting for you."

Instincts kicked in and she sensed their plans. "Sergio, if you're planning some payback on the *Armas* gang at their warehouse tonight, it's not a good idea. Just sayin..."

Now she heard the hesitation from his end. "You're just sayin'. Okay, baby, I'm hearin'. Talk soon."

Cassi sunk to the floor, the wall against her back her support. She let the phone drop and covered her face, her hands trembling so much they barely wiped the tears that flowed in a steady stream.

Desperate to remember the night she'd seen her brother die, she worked at forcing away the gray fog of pain to let her memory replay the scene. She'd been hiding behind some bushes by a fence. The low lights at the back of the warehouse had lit the narrow loading zone and not much else.

She recalled mingling figures standing by the side of the building. The person she'd had her sights on, her brother, had been punched. Before he could retaliate, the others began kicking him. At that point, everything became foggy. Her senses, numb from shock and fear, had frozen.

Frustrated, she banged her fists against her head. *You've got to remember. How can such a traumatic event just fade? What the hell happened then?*

Trying to force the images did the opposite. Frustrated, swiping her cheeks, she rose to her feet and grabbed some paper towels from the dispenser.

Wetting them with cold water, she wiped her eyes and then placed the soggy bulk against the back of her neck and took a few deep breaths like she did for yoga. The discipline of that calmed her and she let her head hang while the earlier scene returned. *What happened next Cass?*

She dove back into the nightmare and once again heard the authorities calling out from her right side for everyone to stop and put their hands up. That's when the shots were fired, a fatal one directed at Raoul.

A curtain of disbelief lifted for a few seconds and she saw again as the bullet jerked his body and he slumped over.

Lord God, I was a witness. And I can't even remember if the assassins had been all men or if there had been a woman there. I hadn't paid any attention to them—only to Raoul.

Useless! I'm less than useless.

Suddenly, she questioned what Sergio had just told her. Wait... how the hell could Juan have been there? Rusty had told her Juan had been in the hospital that night. And if she trusted anyone in the world, it would be her father and brother's old trainer... and her best friend.

Checking her watch, she decided it was too late to call him then. She'd call first thing in the morning. This had to be settled. Besides, it was past time for her to get back to work. It's a wonder Sam hadn't come in here looking for her.

She opened the door only to have another woman push her backwards and follow her in. Shocked, in no way prepared for the bitchiness her attacker displayed, Cass stepped back and waited. Paying close attention, Cass saw it was one of the two who'd been in a clinch upstairs on the dance floor. This chick was about medium height and had a pretty enough face if it hadn't been marred with bitterness and too much fast living.

"You want to stay away from Dani, fuckwit or you'll be answering to me. We're in a relationship and I don't want you sniffing around, trying to get into her pants."

The ridiculousness of the situation struck Cass

and made her grin. "Okay. No problem." The thought of her and Dani being intimate in any way made her shudder with revulsion. *Not in a million years.*

"You think it's funny, bitch? I've seen you twitchin' your ass, working hard to get my woman's attention. Then you go and attack her.... What's up with that shit?" The dark-haired tyrant's green eyes shot hate pellets straight at Cassi and the situation became even more bizarre.

How the hell had things progressed this far? "Look, I don't want any trouble. And I didn't attack Dani on purpose. It was pure reflex when she grabbed my arm. Besides, she understood so just back off, let me by and we'll forget this little chat ever took place."

Instead of listening, the other girl stepped forward and pushed against Cassi's chest. "You think so, huh?" She shoved her again, this time harder. "I don't fucking like you. I want you to leave the club. Call in and quit. Then I'll forget about kicking your skinny ass hard enough to land you in a hospital bed."

Since no one else knew what was happening, Cass tried to play it cool. She'd let the reckless bully have her say and then forget about it. Rather than wiping the floor with the chick, she grabbed her in a hold the idiot couldn't break loose from, pushed her face up against the mirror and talked real nice and slow.

"Get this. Not gonna happen. I like my job. You want me to stay away from Dani, guess that's up to her. I got no interest in the boss other than working for her." Cassi hardened her tone so the other couldn't mistake her meaning. "You come at me again, slut, and you better come prepared because I won't be this nice next time."

Pushing her aside, Cassi left the room and went back to work. She couldn't ignore the stare Sam sent her way. His raised eyebrow spoke volumes... *everything okay?*

Her nod might have soothed his worry if the girl from the bathroom hadn't come up to the counter, slapped it hard till Cass looked her way and then aimed a gesture in her direction.

With one eye closed and her hand held forward, she pretended to shoot Cassi with a make-believe gun.

Chapter
Twenty-two

While he'd been with Cassi, Trace had texted Sam that they needed to meet. Sam waited until Cass got back from wherever she'd disappeared and then walked out for a cigarette break. He showed up a block away.

Trace attacked as soon as the other man approached from out of the dark alley. "You let her go upstairs?"

"Let her? My ass! That chick does whatever the hell she wants to. I was busy with a customer. Next thing I know, she's flipping the boss and one step away from getting her head blown off. Scared the shit out of me." Words burst out as if he'd needed to vent. "Working undercover in a joint like that's bad enough. Having you ride my ass about Cass makes it fucking punishment. She's made another enemy with Andino's slut, Maddy, tonight. The bitch gave Cass a warning that meant business."

Trace felt the pressure as his stomach took another beating. Bile rising, his muscles tightened and pain gripped his insides. His knees bent to take the hit. He growled, his fury reaching the ends of his control. "What happened?"

"I don't know. She came out of the ladies looking messed and the other chick followed her to the bar and gave her the finger." He showed Trace what he meant by that and grabbed Trace's arm as he lurched forward.

"The girl was high, Trace. It could have meant nothing." Sam took a hit from his cigarette and added, "Don't worry, I'll be watching. Cass's good people. I care about her."

"Keep her safe, man." Shaking his head back and forth, a grimace split Trace's face and he swore a litany of cuss words strung together in a way every frustrated guy would understand. Once his heartbeat slowed, he settled down enough to add, "She's bloody dynamite, I know it. Just do the best you can, bro. You're the main reason I don't have heart failure every time she goes in for her next shift."

"Chrissakes, man. If you trust me so much, what's with the reconnaissance, hiding like a love-sick kid at the back of the club? She noticed you tonight. Hell, I see you every time."

Knowing Sam would have made him hadn't stopped Trace from his stupid behavior. How the hell could he stay away when he knew the fucking dangers lurking in that hellhole?

"Talking about her seeing me, she shared some info that human ape Acedo had given her. He said the gang wasn't there because they were at the warehouse working with a shipment that was supposed to be arriving."

Stiffening, his interest peaking, Sam questioned, "Did she say anything else. Like where it was coming from? Or when?"

"No. Just what I told you. Did you guys know about it already?"

"Kind of. We knew they were making preparations for a big haul but Dani kept it quiet about what night it would be happening. Okay, I'll contact the others and we'll get set up for around midnight. Your guys might wanna hang around in case it all goes to hell and we need backup. Just don't get too close until after we move in."

"Already on it. We'll lay low. It's your play. Too bad you can't be in on it yourself."

"Don't I fucking know it." Disgusted, Sam ground out his butt. "My assignment is to dig a lot deeper than one crappy shipment. We need to know whose driving this wagon and I'm beginning to think there had to be a boss one hell of a lot smarter than Dani Andino who set this all up to begin with. That's the dude I want behind bars."

Chapter Twenty-thre e

When Cass left the bar after shift, Sam walked with her to her car to make sure of her safety. "You gonna tell me what went on in the bathroom between you and Maddy?"

"Maddy. Is that her name? Suits her. She's as mad as they come. And I'm not just talking her disposition." Cass giggled, tired as hell, her brain not functioning as it would have without this added stress.

"Hey, Princess, take it from me. That chick isn't a joke. She's one ice cube away from being a fucking glacier."

Breaking up even more, Cass laughed until the tears ran and she had to lean against her car. "You said that on purpose."

Grinning, finally chuckling, Sam nodded. "Yeah

I'm a stand-up. I want you to take me serious, sugar. From what I've heard, she's been working hard to get into it with Dani and now she's gotten her wish. A chick like her, she's not gonna like having anyone hog her territory if you get my meaning."

"Hog her... man, we're talking about a person. Not some piece of land."

"Piece of ass—piece of land, to those weirdos, it's all the same. They care about ownership and will fight to the death if another moves in on what they consider to be their property. Are you getting this, honey?"

"Yeah, I know. I tried telling the dopey slut I had no intentions of getting into a relationship with Dani. Man, what could I say? That I hate the mean-hearted crazy whose always washing her hands with that antibiotic stuff she carries around? She's the big boss. How could I put her down or talk shit about her? So I tried to tell Mad Maddy I wasn't interested. Man these people are so dysfunctional, Sam. I swear I don't know how they live in the real world."

"Hell, sugar. This is their real world. And they know the rules. You're the babe out of water. Just quit making so many waves, okay?"

Chapter
Twenty-four

On the drive home, Cass's cell phone rang and she looked at the caller ID to see who it was, expecting that the person on the line at this hour would be Trace.

With the streets being empty and traffic non-existent, she took a chance and answered it.

"Honey, I'm tied up right now. The FBI hit the *Armas* warehouse tonight and it turned ugly."

Knowing a lot of the boys and liking quite a few, she had to ask. "Was anyone killed?"

"No. Plenty were shot and will be out of commission for a while though. Dani's gonna be pissed. Her shipment is now in police custody and so are crucial members from her gang, some of the bigshots from L.A. It's a mess. Looks like I'll be here at least another hour."

"I'm sorry Trace. I'll miss you." Her voice had dropped, full of the misery she couldn't hide.

116 Mimi Barbour
body

"Believe me, baby, I'll be missing you more. For sure I'll be there to pick you up at four-thirty tomorrow for the funeral."

"Funeral?" Now Cass was stumped.

"You wanted me to go with you to Mani Abel's funeral, remember? Dani had asked you to go for her and the gang."

Stunned that she'd forgotten, she groaned. "Right. I remember now. Yes, the church ceremony starts at five. Thanks for reminding me."

"We'll go straight to my mom's place after that."

"I'm looking forward to it, Trace." She swallowed her disappointment and added, "Babe, don't work too hard tonight."

"Nah! Paperwork isn't deadly just dull. I miss you already, Cassidy Santino. You have no idea... "

The phone went dead and she held on for a few seconds not wanting to end her connection to him.

By the time she got home, she'd accepted she'd be sleeping alone again. Pulling into the driveway, she started up the veranda stairs and found a parcel waiting for her on the porch.

In a medium-sized, plain brown box, no special wrappings, it sat innocuous, safe from any curious neighbors because of its ordinary appearance.

Before picking it up, she glanced around to make sure no one was spying on her. Now that Dani had let Juan back into the club, they'd kept him busy and she'd noticed he hadn't been around the last couple of nights, just the few daytime visits stinking up her bedroom, the sick pervert.

After what Sergio had told her earlier about the possibility of him being at the warehouse the night Raoul died, her aversion for the hairy man had ratcheted up a few more notches and had turned toxic.

If Rusty confirmed his story in the morning, she'd have to let Sergio know he'd made a mistake. But, if her old friend had no proof about Juan being in the hospital during that specific time, she'd pass on this recent info to Trace and let him do his job.

Hope escalated. If he brought Juan in and interrogated him, they might get their answers. She'd tell Trace that Sergio had pressured her to let him take care of Raoul's killer himself. Trace could use that threat to force Juan to confess.

Just the thought had her tingling with pleasure. Maybe if that happened, they could put this all behind them. She could go back to living in her normal world again, where people didn't think like gutter rats and act worse.

Shaking off her doldrums, she carried the parcel into the kitchen and undid the top. When she looked inside, the world stopped.

Chapter
Twenty-five

Nestled in the fold of tissue paper was a porcelain bouquet of gorgeous roses, all red and symbolizing a sweetheart's devotion. The ornament stood about a foot high, the vase dainty and pure white with china flowing ribbons decorating the base.

Cassi had never seen anything more beautiful. Her heart yearned to find Trace's name on the card, which would mean she could adore this precious memento rather than tossing it in the trash with the other flowers.

Hands shaking, she tore off the envelope and found the words *Happy Birthday* in gold script. She pulled out the card and held her breath until she saw the two words at the bottom which released pure joy.

Love, Trace.

He'd remembered that yesterday had been her birthday. How appropriate were his flowers. No doubt, he'd expected to be with her when she'd be opening this gift and sharing in her excitement.

Quickly, she texted her message, *I'll thank you in person. So you know – these roses are the most beautiful gift I've ever received. I love it! xo*

Seconds later, his answer appeared on her screen. *You're very welcome – looking forward to enjoying your appreciation in person. xo.*

After she read his comment, she noticed another text waiting and clicked it open. Sergio's message made her smile.

Paid attention to your warning and glad I did... I owe you... again!

This time she didn't reply.

***

A phone call woke Cass late the next morning and started her day off the way she wished every morning could begin. "Hey, kiddo, I have a surprise waiting for you here at the gym."

"What is it, Rusty?"

"Like I said, it's a surprise, so get your cute little butt down here and see what I got for ya. Then you can buy an old dude some lunch. You up for that?"

"You betcha. I'll be there soon." Cassi glanced over at Trace's roses and caressed them with gentle strokes. The night before, she'd carried her unique present into the bedroom and left it on the bedside table with the nightlight on. It was the last image she'd seen before passing out, exhausted.

Less than an hour later, she sauntered toward

Rusty's only to see a few people, plus Rusty, hovering around a vehicle outside of the gym. Making her way over, she saw they were milling around a motorcycle, a model she was familiar with because she'd been taking lessons on a bike similar. The school's bike was a disgusting green with rust spots. This Kawasaki NINJA RR MONO 250 was silver and black and gorgeous.

She'd memorized that specific info because it was the bike she most wanted to own and train on until she could switch to using Raoul's Harley.

Quickening her stride, she approached; Rusty's wide grin grabbing her attention.

"What do you have there? And why are you looking so smug, Rusty?"

"This crotch rocket's for sale, funny face. The broad who owns it is moving and she's selling it cheap. What do you say? I got it checked over and they took it for a trial run. It's a sweet ride, Cass."

Pure glee ramped up her heartbeats and she felt like a fool standing, nodding, her sentences fragmented showing her excitement. "For me? It's perfect. I love it. I'll buy it. You sweet man."

As she headed toward him, arms spread and hugs written all over her face, the old man removed his tuke and shrunk into himself like a shy kid who knows he can't escape the coming consequence—might as well man up.

"Yeah, yeah. Glad you're happy, monkey." He patted her back and then stepped away; ignoring the snorts and whistles the rest of the group teased him with. "Glad you wore appropriate gear, Cass. You wanna take it out? Take her for a spin and see if you want to keep it."

Excited, revved so high she could barely stop from skipping; so when it came, the disappointment hit her like a sledge hammer. "There's no helmet. I don't have head gear."

During her lessons, it had been drilled into her why she needed to be safe at all times. She'd promised herself to never take chances and end up like the accident victims she'd seen in the videos they'd shown the students as a warning of what does happen to those taking stupid chances.

Flushing, Rusty dashed as fast as his arthritic limbs would take him over to the wall where an open box waited. He picked it up and hurrying back, shoved it forward and let the infrequent grins split his face. "Happy Birthday, brat."

Hands held out front, he backed away. Horror from her tears and reaching arms overcoming the old guy. "You cry all over me and the deal's off, Cassi Santino. I'm warning you."

Smooching another kiss on his scrunched-up cheek, she crowed. "You are the sweetest man alive, you old goat. If you were a couple of decades younger, I'd be hauling you to a magistrate. How you ever escaped from getting caught all these years, I'll never know. A sweetheart like you, it's a pure sin."

Seeing how her words pleased him and given him back a semblance of manly pride, she shoved her bag at him, reached for the helmet, slipped it on and adjusted it. Then she took her stuff and stored it away in the saddlebag.

Waving back at everyone watching and smiling, she sped away and had an hour of unadulterated pleasure before returning and collecting Rusty for the promised lunch treat.

Chapter Twenty-six

Sitting across from her old friend at his favorite lunch bar down the street from the gym, Cassi picked away at the huge basket of fries until they delivered the hamburgers. Inhaling the smell of cooked onions smothering greasy meat, her taste buds resonated with a chorus of Hallelujahs.

The whole time they'd waited for their meal, she'd sung the praises of her new ride and Rusty had sat, nodding. "It's a safe bike for you, brat. A good fit in size and easy to maneuver. You don't need anything else."

Stiffening, she let him down easy. "I promise I'll practice on this one a lot, Rusty. You've always known my dream was to ride Raoul's Harley one day, right?"

Groaning, he shook his head and muttered. "Just like your old man, a pain-in-the-ass stubborn. Okay, you'll do what you gotta do. Just don't come to me for sympathy when you're all smashed up in some hospital."

Cass grinned at the ridiculousness of his statement and reached across to pat his gnarled fingers. "I'll be careful. I need to ask you a question, Rus. But I don't want to ruin the meal. Enjoy, then we'll talk."

A while later, satisfied from the huge lunch and sipping on their drinks, Cass watched Rusty wipe his napkin across his face and to hide a burp.

"What's up, kid?"

"Tell me what you know about Juan Acedo."

Rusty's face wore his surprise in a comical way. His eyes grew larger and his mouth scrunched to one side. "Huh? What do you wanna know about that lowlife for?"

Taking note of his attitude, she continued. "Wasn't he Raoul's friend?"

Rusty took off his tuke and scratched his flattened white hair. Then he glared at her from under bushy eyebrows, his one eye sending a message she needed to pay attention to. "Gang members...they hung out a bit. What's this all about?"

"You told me he couldn't have been with Raoul the night he died because he'd been in the hospital. It's all mixed up in my head now so can you explain again what you said."

"I told you I never believed a freakin' word that came out of his lyin' mouth, is what I told you. And to stay away from the asshole is what else I told ya."

An inkling returned as the words filtered into her memory. Right! Rusty hadn't liked him. She remembered now.

"You told me he missed the funeral because he was in the hospital from a beating for not wanting to hurt Raoul." Eerie foreboding worked on the nerves in her stomach. A frisson of pure hate planted its seed.

"Doll, all I know is what I'd heard. Not sayin' it's true. The word was that he'd refused to be in on teaching Raoul a lesson that night and they'd turned on him instead... put him in the hospital. Now the rumor could have been started by the stupid lame-ass himself, how the hell do I know? All's I can tell you is he didn't show up at the funeral and the next time I seen him, he was a mess."

"Yes. The day I met him, he still looked like he'd gone a few rounds. And that was some time after Raoul had died."

"That's when I called that Detective Maguire to let him know the pric... ahh schmuck had shown up at the gym again... remember?"

Thoughts of Trace lit her insides and the image of them together brought out a blush she didn't have time to hide.

Not being too stupid, Rusty jumped on it before she could change the subject. "What's going on, kiddo? You got a lovesick look on your mug. Kinda like the one your brother wore the last few times I'd seen him."

What! Raoul had been in love?

"Say again, Rusty? He never mentioned a girl to me."

"Yeah, well sisters don't need to know everything. Quit changin' the subject. You tell me why the mention of Maguire got you smirking and blushing."

"We've been seeing each other. He's a good man, Rusty. Has a sick mom he looks after and a job that he takes pride in."

"Doesn't hurt that he's a good-looker too, right?" He grinned when he saw his words had produced more blushes and a prideful expression. "He's got a decent rep in the city, Cass. But remember, cops live hard and fast. It's their job to play in the dirt and many can't brush it off when their shift's over. They're a tough breed, those guys. Not easy to love."

"It's all true, Rus. He's a good guy and I have no choice in how I feel. It just fills me. I'm stuck on him." She reached over and put her hand against his cheek and was delighted when he rubbed his face lightly against the pressure.

"What about you, Rus? Ever had an inkling to settle down and get married, have kids?"

"Nah! Lived fast and loose when I was younger and never met a girl I'd trust my life with. Being a boxer is hard on the chicks too. Now I'm too beaten up to give a damn. Guess the one thing I might be sorry for is not having a daughter like you." He winked with his good eye.

Grinning, she replied, "So, you can adopt me now. I'm available."

"Consider it done, monkey." He reached across with his hand extended and waited for her to place hers there. Then he shook as if a deal had been cemented. Warmth filled her and she glowed from his gentleness. Her love for her old friend swelled, filling all those spaces where emptiness had existed.

Rather than embarrass him with further demonstrations of her affection, she retreated to the earlier subject that tweaked her sisterly conscience. "Tell me, Rus, did you know anything about Raoul's girlfriend? You said he looked like there might have been a love interest."

"Yeah. When I teased him about it, he got kinda angry. Said she wasn't a female I'd approve of. Then he added, what a person did wasn't always who they were inside. Never understood what he was driving at. The boy didn't look proud like you do. He looked more conflicted... and miserable."

"Did he ever tell you her name?"

"No. But he had a picture of her he showed me once. A pretty filly with long blonde hair and a face full of sorrow."

Shit!

Cass had promised to stay away from upstairs at

the club. Now it looked like she'd be breaking her
word.

Chapter Twenty-seve n

Preparing for her date with Trace later, Cassi had to grin. One day they would tell their grandchildren their first date was to a funeral. She chuckled and continued rinsing the soap off in the shower.

Bursting into song, she sang along with the music from her wireless speaker she had hooked up to her favorite radio station through Bluetooth. Not expecting visitors, her front and back door locked, when a hand reached in behind the plastic curtain and touched her, she freaked.

Before she could react, arms tightened around her, lifted her off her feet and a gentle voice whispered sweetness into her ear.

"Whoa, baby. It's me. Calm down. I don't wanna get hurt." His harsh chuckle broke into her reaction and as soon as he lowered her, she whirled into his arms.

Body slippery from the hot water raining down on them, she clutched him with a serious frown on her face. "God, you scared me." She pounded his back a few times before caressing the same place. "Call out next time."

"I wanted to surprise you. It wasn't until I'd made the move that I realized with you, that might not be such a smart idea." With both hands he smoothed the dripping hair from her cheeks and kissed her lips, his tongue searching for hers and playing with it when she obliged.

Hard, wanting, his body teased hers just by its very nudging presence and she moaned with passion. "What a wonderful idea!"

"Humm... I know. Got away earlier than I thought, caught a few winks and decided to check on you and see if you were ready. Imagine my glee when I found you were... ahh not only ready but naked and so damn pretty."

Giggling softly, she kissed his neck. His mouth found her lips while his fingers found another opening and pleasured her there as well.

Following his example, she used her hands to delight the man whose moan turned to whispers of love words before he pushed her against the wall and lifted her legs around his waist.

Plunging into her soaked passage, Trace moaned as her body gripped his slick and tight. Hungrily, she found his lips again and let his kiss lift her to the dizzying heights she knew preluded an approaching orgasm.

Intoxicated with his randy lust; her breasts swelled from his fondling and her nipples puckered. He sucked at each until they sent signals to her lower body that made it tighten. Deep inside, the pulsations began in earnest. His seductive squirming, burying himself deeper inside with each plunge created shudders and spasms of pure, unstoppable satisfaction.

A husky litany of loving words delighted her and she responded to him with her own urging. "Yes, Trace. I love it. Yes. Please. *Harder*."

The last word broke the spell he'd been under of gentle sensitive seduction. Now he pumped into her, his groin hammering against her welcoming body.

Panting, drenched, she shattered. Her intense climax lingering, lasting forever. Drained, her nerve ends tingling deliciously; she tightened her muscles and relished his wild, hot shuddering.

Slowly, lowering her so she stood in front, he leaned his arms over her head against the shower walls. She knew his knees must be as weak as hers and she let him have the few moments he needed to gain his strength back. Meanwhile, she reached for the soap and began lathering his chest, her hands working through the hair with gentle strokes and then over his shoulders and around to his back.

Overcome with love, she took the time to hug him hard.

"Baby, you sure you want to fan the flames? What you do to this poor fellow is pitiful. Yet he can't help it."

Not sure if he was talking about himself in third person or his growing protrusion, she laughed and loved it when he grinned his good-natured way and then hugged her hard. Satiated, they washed each other and seeing the hour had passed, they rushed to be on time for the ceremony that Cass had promised to attend.

Chapter Twenty-eigh t

This service was like most of the others Trace had been to. And in his job, he'd attended quite a few. Because they were late, they stood behind the last row not wanting to disturb anyone having to make way for them.

After the mass, the priest took time to do the eulogy and then some of the family spoke on Mani's behalf.

Not being able to concentrate, Trace's mind returned instead to the pleasure he'd just experienced with the enticing little witch standing by his side. Pretty in her pink sundress, her hair pinned up with a fancy clip holding the one side in place so it couldn't drop down to hide her face, she made him proud and he knew he beamed with delight.

She'd added a lacy black shawl to wear during the church portion and he felt it such a shame for her to cover up what he found so attractive.

Close together, he reached down between them and slipped his hand around hers and loved that her fingers connected without hesitation. The loving smile she flashed his way warmed his innards to pure mush. Their eyes met knowingly and he had to force himself not to bend over to kiss her. As if she knew his thoughts, the cheeky devil winked before turning back to the front.

As expected, the deceased's family appeared heartbroken. They looked to be immigrants who'd been in the US for a couple of generations, not newcomers to the country. The stoic mother, appearing as a business woman, seemed well-groomed like a professional. The father seemed less sophisticated, noticeably bewildered and more upset. His sobs could be heard during personal sections of the ceremony.

The dark-haired girl who stood near kept her arm around his shoulders and patted his back from time to time. Since her silhouette was too far away to identify, he didn't pay her much attention.

It wasn't until she turned to help the older man back up the aisle that he felt Cassi stiffen and he saw the two girls' eyes connect.

Arlene!

Recognizing the fighter from the boxing match the night before, he tried to remember her last

name and it wouldn't come to him. Wait... it wasn't
Abel. It was Montgomery. Nevertheless, his mind
reacted. What the hell was she doing at Mani
Abel's funeral as a family member?

Once the congregation who'd gathered outside
were all heading to the church annex where they'd
set up a luncheon, Cassi and Trace followed. Not
speaking, they seemed of one mind. Trace had no
doubt that Cassi's intentions were to corner
Arlene and find out why she had been sitting at the
front with Mani's father.

Working their way to where his relatives sat in a
semi-circle, Trace and Cass held back to let others
share their condolences.

Meanwhile, different ladies waylaid them with
trays of ice tea and dainties so they helped
themselves and visited with a few of the guests
who stopped to make them welcome and pass the
time.

One woman had more to say then some of the
others. From the sneering expression on her made-
up face that tried to appear twenty years younger
and had the opposite effect, she cornered them so
there was no escape.

"How did you know Mani?"

"He was a friend of my brother's, "Cassi
answered before Trace would be forced to admit
his professional position.

Disgust filled the other's face and her abrasive
attitude pissed Trace off royally. "Is your brother

also one of those gang members that sell drugs to the young and do those terrible drive-by shootings? I warned Barbara, Mani's mother, about his goings-on. She never did have control on that boy and she has even less hold on that girl they took in as a baby. Darn shame when families are forced to deal with other family member's mistakes. The slut, Phil's sister, lacked restraint and had the morals of a bitch in heat. Barbara's husband, who has a soft heart to match his soft head, forced Barbara to let the little bastard live with them."

Trace's intuition kicked in. "Are you referring to Arlene Montgomery? She's a family member?"

"That's what I said. Her mother, the immoral sinner, dropped her baby off one day and they never heard tell of her since. Left the brat for Barbara and Phil to raise." The gossipy old witch shook her head, disgust clear in a face where her mouth lines formed a downward spiral – no doubt because her lips never curved up in the other direction. Cranky old bitch!

He made an excuse and they left her side as quickly as they could politely get away. Seeing an opportunity to give their respects to the parents, Trace guided Cassi over and watched her in action.

Bending close so her words wouldn't be overheard, Cassi spoke first to her gym partner. "I'm sincerely sorry for your loss, Arlene. Mani was a nice guy. He used to joke around with me at the club but was always a true gentleman." Thinking her phrase damn quaint for today's kind of society, he had to remember Cassi was a librarian when he'd met her. Go figure, his little spitfire working in a library?

Arlene, uncomfortable with having to be civil, nodded and murmured one word, "Thanks."

Before they could move along, Mani's father leaned over and added, "Leni and Mani were inseparable, especially when she was a baby. He was thrilled to have a little sister and even though they were cousins, you wouldn't know it by the way he treated her. Right, Leni?" He reached for her hand, his trembling from emotion. Arlene moved fast to grasp his fingers and answered, "Yes Uncle. Mani looked after me my whole life."

A scowl appeared as she turned to stare up at Cassi and then she shifted her look to him so he felt the icy intimidation. "He didn't deserve to die."

Before he could answer, Cassi did it for him. Her tone as cold as Arlene's attitude, she said, "Neither did my brother, Raoul."

As soon as the words left her mouth, Cassi had turned away and marched to the exit, her head held high and her hands clenched by her side. She hadn't stuck around to see Arlene's reaction. He had. The girl looked as if she'd been slugged with a baseball bat.

Chapter
Twenty-nine

Cassi couldn't seem to shake the bad taste Arlene's words had produced. Her mind played them over and over all the way to Trace's home. That Arlene could so easily dismiss her brother's death had lowered the girl even more in her opinion. In the past, she'd often forced herself to put up with Arlene's stubborn eccentricities, her refusal to let anyone inside her barriers or to even be civil.

If only Rusty didn't have so many plans for the future of his business wrapped up in her talent. The one boxer that could elevate his place, put him in the limelight, bring in a lot more customers and fulfill his dream for having a thriving gym. Without the love she felt for that old man, she'd have dumped the ornery chick right at the start.

However, Rusty meant everything to her. She'd take on the world for him. So if it meant putting up with that bitchy brat, she'd handle it the best she could. But for Arlene to hit below the belt like she'd done today, Cassi decided enough was enough. No way she'd get back in the ring with that sleaze. She'd explain to Rusty, he'd understand. Let Arlene find another sparring partner.

"Earth to Cassidy, we're here. The whole way here you've been off in your own little world. Anything I can do?"

Shaking off her snit, Cass sighed and then laughed. "Cassidy back to earth, I'm fine. Just didn't like the way Arlene spoke to me. I got the feeling her message was personal – that she thought Raoul's death didn't matter like Mani's. That in her mind, he did deserve to die."

"Just so you know, when you said your piece and then walked away, she looked stunned. Before you get pissy about her, you might want to check into this a bit more."

"What're you implying? That she didn't know about Raoul's death?"

"No. That wouldn't make any sense. Working-out at the same gym he did, she would have seen him there. People would have talked about him getting shot. I don't know, baby. Just sayin'... your remark stunned the shit out of her. "

Cassi pondered his statement. Arlene treated her like shit and she didn't pal with anyone at Rusty's. In fact, the only person she'd even seen her behave half decent with was the trainer himself and even with him, she pushed the limits of respect.

She had the words on the tip of her tongue to tell Trace about seeing the *Armas* tattoo on Arlene's back and how she'd had the ink reworked into a different pattern. But he stopped her in the best way possible.

He leaned over and kissed her and within a very short time, rather than a playful tribute, it became hot and heavy. Noticing his breathing had thickened; she pushed against his chest and leaned her forehead against his chin.

"Are you sure you want to stroke the fires again. You know how combustible we are when we're together."

He breathed deeply, the ragged sound making her grin. "Right. We'll save it for later."

"Right. Then I'll be naked and wet, squirming with need, ready to—"

"God have mercy! Did anyone ever call you a brat?"

"Now that you mention it, I recall numerous times." Giggling, she reached in the back for the huge bouquet of flowers she'd gotten him to stop for and stepped out of the car. Then she waited for his slower exit while he adjusted his pants.

As soon as he reached her side, he smacked her playfully on the butt and then wrapped his arm around her waist while guiding her to the front door.

***

Trace couldn't believe how well his mom looked as she greeted them from her wheelchair at the door. She appeared more youthful, full of energy, kinda like the old days when she'd chase him around the house, grab him in a hold and kiss all over his face until he'd beg for pity.

That was the woman he'd adored all his life. The mother who had always put his needs first. She'd given him the gift of patience, trust and admiration, never belittling his efforts. Instead, she'd spurred him on to be the best man he'd ever envisioned.

Kathleen reached for Cassi's hand even before he'd had a chance to make the introductions. "You must be Cassi, the girl who's made my son happier than I've ever seen him. I've been wanting to thank you. As a doting mama, I couldn't be happier."

"And you must be the same mother he adores and lights up every time he talks about you."

Kathleen swung to her son and lifted a finger to wag in his direction. "Trace, how many times do I have to tell you that bragging isn't polite?"

"Unless it's about you..."

Kathleen grinned. "Right!" She winked at Cassi. "That's true. I forgot that part." She curled her finger back into her fist and laughed. Reaching out, she waved toward the woman entering from the hallway. "Cassi, I'd like to introduce my nurse, Mrs. Devin. She likes us to call her Mary."

Cassi stepped forward with her hand extended.

"I'm pleased to meet you, Mary. I know your son, Juan."

Obvious pride lit her face as she corrected Cassi. "Yes, my adopted son. He's been a life-sav... *ahem* a joy to me in my old age. I don't know how I'd survive without him."

Once settled in the living room, Trace gestured for the ladies to stay while he went into the kitchen, following the fabulous stream of good smells that tickled his taste buds.

Sure enough, when he lifted the lid off the pot on the stove, he knew his mom had made the spaghetti sauce he loved.

The noodles were on the counter, ready and waiting to be cooked, no doubt homemade like she knew he loved. He pulled out the pitcher of ice tea she'd always kept ready in the fridge and the red wine he knew would go perfect with his favorite meal.

Returning to serve the ladies, he loved watching his mom grin at a comment Cassi had made and then laugh as all three women joined in. He didn't know how she'd pulled this off, how she'd managed to be so well today. He blessed God first, Nurse Mary and whatever new pills they'd found for her to take.

***

Right from the moment she'd met her, Cassi loved Trace's mom. The woman lived in today's world, knew what life was like out there for people nowadays and not just what it had been like in her time. Because of that, it was possible to talk to her like a peer.

As soon as Trace headed for the kitchen, the pretence faded and she saw how hard Kathleen had to work for this deception tonight. She rushed to kneel beside her and reached for her hand. "Love, should you be out of bed? We'd be happy to be with you in the bedroom where you can lie down and be more comfortable."

"Bless you, sweetie. I wanted this night for Trace to remember. He's been so antsy about today, called me more than once to see if we needed him, if he could help. The boy's nuts about you, sugar and it's done this old broad good to see him so happy. You'll treat him right, promise me."

Cassi caught the older woman's piercing look and didn't turn away. "I promise, I'll be as good to him as he'll let me. I love your son very much."

Kathleen's eyes narrowed. "Enough to give up looking for your brother's killer?"

Stunned, Cassi fell back so her butt landed on the floor next to the wheelchair.

"Never mind, I can see the answer in your eyes. Poor Trace! He'll be replacing his mule-headed old mom with a stubborn new wife. Serves him right! That boy never did appreciate anything that came too easy."

Chapter
Thirty

Cassi enjoyed the rest of the evening immensely even if they had to end it early. When she knew Trace's mother had surpassed her strength limitations and was suffering a lot of pain, Mary shared a silent affirmation with her... *Time to go.*

Kathleen's face had lost its color, much of it applied with a liberal hand using makeup no doubt. And her voice had weakened; same as her neck muscles. When she thought no one noticed, the woman vibrated with waves of pain. She'd eaten tiny bits to seem as if she joined in the meal with them, although Cassi knew most of the food had returned on the fork to her plate.

When saying good-bye, she reached to hug the older woman and stopped in time as she caught the negative warning shake from Mary. Instead, she leaned over and placed a soft kiss on her cheek.

"Can I come and see you again? You did promise

me the recipe for your spaghetti sauce."

"Hell, Cass, you can move in and live with me if you want. With that husky voice and your gentle ways, I could have you around me day and night. Whenever you have the time, please come."

Trace turned to Mary. "You look tired, Mary. I'll drop Cassi off at her place and come back to help you clean the kitchen so you're not up too late."

"No. Please don't. You helped me rinse and stack everything earlier so I thought I'd just leave the rest till the morning and fill the dishwasher then. I intend to see to your mom so she can have a peaceful night."

Cassi saw Trace turn away as if overcome from the words Mary had spoken. She knew from what he'd told her, his mother hadn't had any peace for quite some time. It had gotten so the medications couldn't override the agony altogether and no matter what they did, his mother suffered.

Just then Kathleen caught her eye and gestured her closer. The messages she sent drove straight to Cassi's heart. The sick woman touched her hand and it was as if she'd spoken the words. "Take care of Trace... Love him." And then she mouthed, "Thank you."

Chapter
Thirty-one

Cassi held Trace's hand on the way back her place. Neither spoke. The sadness was too raw. She glanced out of the window and saw that he'd taken the wrong turn. She looked at him and he sent her a half smile, gave a brief shake of his head and shrugged. "Bear with me."

"Always." Squeezing his fingers, she settled back against her seat, sighed when he opened both their windows and breathed in the warm desert night air.

This was one of her favorite times of the day. The sweltering sun had replaced its fiery blaze with the splendor of a dazzling sunset. Streaks of purple fought for advantage against billowing clouds of golden brilliance. The blue of the night sky peeked through here and there, a backdrop to remind one of Mother Nature's manipulations to impress her admirers.

Cass enjoyed the wonderful silence, the peace she experienced being surrounded by the beauty from the outside world. Saturated in the love oozing from the man who gently squeezed her hand, she sent up a prayer as a thank you for her blessings.

The calm inside her soul started a song in her heart. It had been such a long time since she'd experienced such sensations and she soaked in the impressions.

Trace had decided to drive through the strip, not a section of the city she tended to visit very often. The night-life had always amazed her, the people crowding, laughing, enjoying themselves was solace to her happy spirit.

Many of the tourists gambled away money they didn't have, couldn't afford. They lived the life of fantasy for just a few days and went home poorer yet strangely satisfied for having had a time-out from reality.

Swinging her head from side to side, she let the fairy-tale from the vivid lights, continuous noise and unparalleled magic soak in. When he pulled into the Paris's underground parking, she grinned her approval.

Soon they strolled amongst the others through the casino, hand in hand, her side glued to his.

"Want a drink?" Leaning close to her ear, he spoke in a soft voice. "Sure." She followed him to the bar stools and perched up on the one to his left.

There were poker machines inserted into the bar in front of them and she watched as he withdrew his wallet, took out a twenty and then placed it in the machine closest to her. "What are you doing? I don't know how to play these games?"

"Haven't you ever played blackjack or poker?"

"Sure, in university as a lark. Never for money."

"Where did you go to school?"

"UNLV. What about you?"

"Same. But I would have already graduated by the time you got there. You're how old?"

Playful, her eyes twinkling, she shook her head. "A lady never tells." The fear he might think her too young for him slammed into her and she didn't intend to take a chance.

He winked. "I have your date of birth on the police report, remember? I know you're in your late twenties and I'm thirty-five. Just perfect, right?"

"Right." Relieved they'd passed an imaginary hurdle, she watched as he played the first game and won. "Okay, show me again how this Blackjack thing works."

Laughing, him teasing, stealing kisses and her immersed in his charming good mood, they spent the next couple of hours having the time of their lives and coming away with a printout that read forty-six cents which he left on the bar for the lady next to him.

Hungry again, they wandered behind the casino area along the cobbled Parisian streets to settle for a treat of crepes that smelled delicious but not near as good as they tasted. Hers – smothered with cinnamon apples and real cream – had her eyes closing while she shoveled in piece after piece.

"You're enjoying that way too much not to let me have a taste. If it's that good, I need to know."

"I'll share mine if you share yours." She waited, delighted when he pretended to think about it.

First he raised his eyebrow as if pondering the question of the ages. Finally he cut off a tiny sliver, picked it up on his fork and aimed it toward her.

"Are you kidding me? That's not gonna get you any of mine, which, by the way, is delicious. Best thing I've ever eaten. Yummy good. Needs to be tasted to be believ—".

"Alright! Okay." He interrupted her mischievousness and scooped up a huge amount of his seafood choice so that she had trouble swallowing it all at once. Then he laughed at her for having to use her napkin to stop it from dropping on her dress.

Stuffed and still delighting in each other's company, they made their way to his vehicle. Once there, he guided her to the passenger side and before he opened her door, he stared into her eyes, his searching for permission. Her need must have flashed because he took his time lowering his lips all the while watching for her reaction, passing a message from his heart to hers. *Lady I want you!* Without words, she answered him. *"I'm all yours."*

His lips searched, gently, slowly tasting, not quite adding the pressure she craved. It was the most seductive kiss he'd given her to date and every nerve in her body reacted to the thrilling sensations it created.

Light-headed, pulsations erupting, breasts tightening, a tide of passion welling, she clutched him closer and her arms around his back tightened, gripped.

Control weakening, it was gut-wrenching when the ring-tone she'd begun to recognize broke the spell. Shivers of apprehension scuttled over her body and slammed her down to earth.

They stared at each other and she could see the fear plastered over his face. It was as if he knew...

Chapter
Thirty-two

That night, Arlene hung in with her uncle until he'd settled. Making her way to the front room where her Aunt Barbara relaxed in a comfy robe, along with her laptop computer and her favorite brand of vodka, Arlene muttered, "I'm off."

"He's sleeping?"

"What do you care?"

Barbara Abel swung her office chair to confront her niece, her face sneering, her expression ugly with grief. "Don't get pissy with me, Leni. Answer my question."

Backing off as she'd always done, Arlene answered. "Yeah. He's asleep."

Surprisingly chatty, no doubt because she'd drank enough to put her in the zone, her aunt spoke again before Arlene had the chance to stomp away. "The service went well today. Most of my employees at the Real Estate office showed up."

Pride rang in her voice and Arlene knew to keep the peace, she'd be expected to compliment her aunt's success. Unable to tell the truth that she had no doubt her aunt's decree that they attend protected their jobs, she added. "Yes. I guess they wanted to support you. Also, some of the relatives did too."

"From your uncle's side. None of mine appeared. Thank God."

Not knowing what to say, Arlene started to edge toward the door and her aunt's next words stopped her in her tracks. "My son's dead because of you. I hope you realize that."

"Excuse me?" Stunned at the frontal attack, more used to innuendos and sarcastic hints, Arlene staggered.

"You heard me." Barbara turned her fury on full force and let it rip. "Mani would never have joined that gang if it weren't for you. He did it to save your ass. We both know it's true so don't try and lie your way out of it."

Stunned by her vehemence, Arlene swallowed hard and slid to the seat behind her legs so she wouldn't end up on the floor. "He told you that?"

"Not really. I overheard him talking on the phone one night when I came down to get a refill and he didn't know I was around. I don't know who he was talking to but what he said was as clear as the nose on your face. He'd joined that bunch of perverted youths to protect you. He said once

Dani had driven out the big boss, he'd work his way close to her. No problem getting to be second in command because the others were a bunch of idiots and he was way smarter. Then he intended to orchestrate a way to buy you out." Her aunt stumbled from her chair closer to where Arlene had collapsed. She stood over her, threatening, eyes full of pain. "Do you disagree?"

"How can I? I didn't know. He never shared with me. In fact, with us having different last names, he kept our relationship hidden so no one could use it against him or me."

Stung, her aunt's voice rose. "We explained why we didn't legally adopt you. Your mother took off. We had no idea how to find her. We had no papers giving us the right. If you want to blame anyone, blame the bitch who named you, left and never looked back."

"Trust me, I do." Although Arlene knew defending herself would get her nowhere with her aunt in this condition, she had to give it a shot. "Some time ago, I went to Dani Andino, the leader, and told her I wasn't cut out for gang life and wanted her to let me leave. She laughed, kicked my ass and told me to get back to the warehouse."

That night of shame had never left Arlene. It was what had driven her to Rusty's gym. Why she'd worked so hard to be able to win in a fight. Dani would get hers one day soon. She was close. Thanks to Cass, her training had paid off.

"You're telling me he didn't share his plans, with you his *petite hermana?*"

Sick inside from her aunt disparaging what to her and Mani had been his sweet way of making her feel that she belonged, she hid her face searching for the hard shell to crawl back behind. The one she tended to shed when in her uncle's affectionate presence.

Finding the cold, dead place she'd been hiding since she'd recovered from Dani's harsh treatment, she bolted to her feet so her aunt had to step back. "Why do you always belittle Mani's affection for me? Did you have to be so jealous?"

"Jealous? Of you? Don't be silly. You just weren't that important. What mattered was my son's future and you stole that from him. He had plans to go to college to get his teaching degree. You messed with all of that—"

Sickened by her aunt's delusions, she yelled, "No. He never wanted that teaching degree you ranted on about. His plans were to open a shop where he'd use his painting talents with an airbrush. He dreamed of personalizing motorcycles and cars for whoever could afford his prices."

"That stupid scribbling. It would never have supported him. I told him that, begged him to quit following dreams and get his feet on the ground."

"So that's why you refused to give him the money for art school." With her legs threatening to collapse, Arlene sat back down, the weight of her aunt's delusions on her thin shoulders.

"Of course. And I told his father if he tried to go behind my back, I'd leave him without a cent to his name. That old man's been living off of my success for years." She turned back to the bottle at the edge of the desk and poured herself another tumbler full of forgetfulness.

Arlene hated the venom in her aunt's tone. She'd heard it aimed in her direction for as long as she could remember. A couple of years ago, she'd suffered one too many insults and took off.

Mani searched until he found her involved with the *Armas* gang, taking more drugs than was safe and living in a way she'd hated. The only people who'd treated her with any vestige of kindness had been Sunshine and later, Raoul Santino.

When Mani'd made the deal with that she-devil, Dani, to let her go free, she hadn't realized he'd traded places for her. And it wasn't until recently that she'd surfaced from her own dark hell to go on living. And Rusty had been the reason she'd managed it.

One day, wandering the streets, tiring herself on purpose so she'd be able to sleep after working all night as an office cleaner, she'd stumbled onto his gym and decided to pay for a few hours work out. The minute she'd stepped inside the joint, the smell, the vibe, everything about the place had screamed home—as if in another life, she'd belonged there.

At first, Rusty had ignored her. She'd stumbled around, watching how others hit the punching bags and speed bags until one day he'd come and ragged her ass. Showed her the best way to use the weights and how she needed her feet to keep up with her arms, the balance and rhythm.

He'd seen something in her she'd never before experienced—a killer instinct and not only for survival. It was the challenge to be the best.

Because she was fucked up, mad at the world, she'd done her best to keep him at arm's length and then later on, Cass. And it worked. They put up with her. No one liked her and she couldn't care less.

Her aunt returned. Appearing nonchalant and failing, she again sagged into the chair facing Arlene. Her hand trembled like most drunks after their limit. With her makeup removed and hundreds of bottles of vodka medications later, her sixty-five years of living appeared obvious in each wrinkle and disgruntled frown line.

"Where are you living?"

"What do you care?"

"I don't. But your uncle does. He has stomach cancer and not a long time left."

Crushed, she couldn't hide the tears. A hard mass of pain settled into her stomach while a headache made itself known. Fighting for the next breath, she asked, "How long has he got?"

"Doctors say a few months. Not that you'd

know. Since you disappeared, we had no idea where you'd gone. Mani was looking for you everywhere."

"He knew where I was. We talked. He cared enough to respect my wishes not to live at home. And... he never mentioned Uncle Phil's illness." *Mani...*

"Well Mani didn't share his knowledge of your whereabouts with me or your uncle either. If Phil hadn't recognized you sneaking into the church, we still wouldn't have known if you were alive or dead from an overdose in some flea-bitten hotel off the strip. Now he's seen you, he'll be after me constantly for you to come home or at the very least, spend more time with him."

Arlene sensed a weakness in her aunt's tirade. As if the woman wanted to force her back into their lives and couldn't ask, couldn't bring herself to show her need of help for her husband.

During the earlier years, growing up in this family, Arlene had seen the huge love between her aunt and uncle fade. Once her aunt started her real estate business and her uncle had lost his cleaning company, things had deteriorated. Now she sensed a strange vulnerability within her aunt's request.

The woman still cared about her husband and was willing to put up with Arlene for his sake. She just didn't know how to ask.

"I won't move back into this house."

"Fine. I'm glad."

Was there a shadow of sorrow behind her sneer? Stunned, Arlene hesitated before speaking again. But then her words burst out, "What do you want from me?"

Tears now streaming, her aunt forced her bottom lip under her teeth to stop it from quivering. Her chin, not having any pressure to stem the tide of her emotion, shook visibly. "I-I think you should come and see us-him. He ne-needs you now that Ma-Mani's gone."

Arlene heard the fear her aunt hadn't been able to hide. The woman had just lost a son and soon she'd be losing her husband. Arlene was the one person left to cling to, the girl she'd ignored while growing up in a house that had never been her home.

On the other hand, Barbara hadn't ever been physically cruel. Arlene—Leni to them, had had nice clothes, good food and her own bedroom. She'd never wanted for anything and her uncle and cousin had more than made up for the love her aunt withheld.

"I can do that. Is there any time you'd rather I came around. Like when you'll be out of the house?"

Flinching, her aunt shook her head. "Doesn't matter. I've been working more and more from home. We have a care-giver who comes in during the hours I'm with my clients or at the office. If it's so important for you not to see me, call first."

Spilling her drink in her haste to leave the room, Barbara finally just let the glass drop to the floor. Staggering her way up the stairs, she ignored the crash of the glass against the ceramic tiles. "Lock the door when you leave."

Arlene watched the still slim woman, short blonde hair immaculately groomed, disappear into the upstairs hallway. How many times had she wished for just one small hug or even an endearment?

Cleaning up her aunt's mess, tears mixing with the alcohol puddled around her, she wondered for the millionth time. Why had her mother dumped her like a pack of unwanted dirty wash on the steps of her uncle's home?

Every time she'd begged her uncle for an explanation, he'd been vague and reassuring. "We assured your mother we'd love to have you; that we'd take care of you like you were our own. I've told you about my parents, how they'd both been killed in a car accident. She and I were the only two left in the family. So, of course, when she found out she was pregnant and the guy couldn't marry her, she came to me for help. That's what big brothers do for their little sisters, like Mani takes care of you. It's just the way things are."

"Why didn't she come back for me?"

"I don't know, Sweetheart. She disappeared and we never heard from her again. You know I tried to find her but..."

"And my dad?"

"Never did find out who she fell in love with. He didn't step up and so we wrote him off."

Arlene left the house and went through the garage, stopping when she got to Mani's Harley. Fingering the bike's keys her uncle had given her, she crouched down to see his latest work. Airbrushed with the dragons he loved painting, she ran her fingers over the intricate designs and wiped the tears away as they dripped. Then she maneuvered the machine out of the side door and far enough down the alley so it wouldn't wake the neighborhood.

Crying hard now, she got on the motorcycle and sent up her thanks that against her uncle and aunt's wishes, Mani had taught her to ride years before. Many of her best times were behind him as he'd ridden them both through the desert.

Oh, Mani. God! I'm so sorry...

Chapter Thirty-three

Trace had dropped Cassi off and then went home to where peace now reigned. Mary greeted him at the door with a hug and led him to Kathleen's bedroom, leaving as soon as he entered.

The room looked neat and he appreciated that she'd straightened everything. She'd even sprayed the room with his mother's preferred lavender scent to cover up the smells he'd connected to her illness.

His tiny mother looked happy in the end. Her face was peaceful. The covers pulled up under her arms and her hands folded over the top as if placed there on purpose.

The huge array of medications gracing her night table seemed superfluous now. She'd never need them again, making her violently sick, stopping the torture for a measly few hours reprieve.

No more watching her life drain away a painful

slow inch at a time. Or seeing the woman he cherished replaced by the suffering skeleton who'd waited each tortuous day for her body to give up the fight.

He spent an hour with her, remembering the good times. When she'd cook him his favorite dishes like she had tonight, no doubt mostly carried out from her instructions and Mary's labour.

He'd worshipped the woman who'd been his biggest fan all his life. Not only when he'd played sports, but all through his police academy training and then when he'd written for his detective's badge. She'd pushed him to work hard, and in the end, she'd been right. He loved his work as she knew he would.

Over the years, they'd had a lot of good times and he'd miss the hell outta her. But... he had Cassi now.

His gut clenched to think that one day when they had a family; his mother wouldn't be there to help raise the grandkids. She'd have loved that. He kissed her forehead and then the hand he clenched, sliding it under the cover so she wouldn't be cold.

Feeling like a huge weight of worry had been replaced with a much smaller amount of self-pity, he wiped his face. Then he went to the kitchen fridge to grab a beer. Of the three he'd noticed earlier, one was missing. Confused, he shook his head. Who knew Mary had a taste for the stuff?

Joining the nurse where she'd sat crocheting while waiting for him in the living room, he flung himself into his chair and smiled at her worried expression. She'd made a pot of tea and picking it up, she refilled her cup. "It's a blessing. You do understand."

"I'm sad to say, it's what I've been hoping would happen for some time now. I'll admit that I'm glad she's finally resting easy. You can call 911 and let them know she's passed on. They'll send a coroner to sign the death certificate and then she can be taken to this funeral home." He handed her a card. "I've made all of the arrangements. They know what to do once she arrives."

"I'll do that, Trace. Don't worry. I've been through this a number of times. Unfortunately, all of my patients end up like this. It's the worst part of my job. Many times, I've wished for miracles."

Trace stood to leave. "You were my miracle, Mary. Mom was happy with you in charge. And I needed a nurse with a kind heart to take care of her."

The older woman gave him a gentle smile and stood to follow him to the door. "I love my patients, Trace. I always make sure they're looked after at the end."

Chapter Thirty-four

Cassi mourned for Trace. She'd seen firsthand how Kathleen suffered and had no doubt the woman had prayed for release from the world where no amount of joy could offset the brutality of her life.

Cassi had also seen the way Trace had reacted to Mary's announcement. After ending the call, he'd hugged her hard. Then he'd breathed a huge sigh, smiled down into her face and laid his forehead against hers. "Mom's pain is over. She's comfortable now."

"That's good, love. From what you told me, it's been a long battle."

After he'd dropped her off at the house, she'd gone to bed where she dozed; waiting for him in case he needed to be with her.

A few hours later, she heard the key in the lock. Thankful that he'd seen where she kept her hidden key, she knew he'd replace it before coming inside.

That gave her time to turn on the bedside lamp and plump the pillow on his side.

Except that he never appeared.

She called out. "Trace, honey. I'm in the bedroom."

Still no answer

Then she knew. Trace hadn't returned.

With slow steps, holding her breath, she crept from the bed and inched her way to the door, listening for footsteps in the hall.

Nothing.

A faint whiff from a joint drifted to her and she knew who her visitor was. "Juan. If you're still in my house, I'm gonna kick your ass."

No answer.

Deciding she wouldn't hide away like a frightened child, she stepped into the living room and in the dark; she saw the red glow from the next drag.

Considering she shook all over, her voice sounded steady. "Get out."

"No can do. I need a friend tonight, Cass. I won't hurt you. I just need a friend."

Not sure why she believed him, she just did. Uncomfortable with his considering her as a friend, she couldn't fault him for thinking it was the case. Since she'd portrayed that role their last time together at the club, he had the right. "Fine, I'll get dressed and make some coffee. Wait here."

She hurried back to her room, grabbed

underwear, jeans and a T-shirt and locked herself into the bathroom to change. Then she went into the kitchen and made two coffees which she brought to the darkened room. Placing them on the table, she reached to turn on the light.

"Don't... Please."

Glad she'd left on the kitchen light so it wasn't completely dark, she hesitated. Following her instincts from the weird note in his voice, she did as he asked. "What's wrong, Juan?"

In a childlike way, he answered. "I felt sad and I had no one to be with."

"What about your mom? Couldn't you have gone to her?"

"No." He barked the word and then sensing he'd overreacted, he added. "She's on a case."

"She'd still be there for you when you feel like this."

"Not if it's her fault I feel like this. I don't want to talk about it."

"What about other friends? I'm sure there are people in your life you hang out with?"

"I used to like a girl called Leni. She left me. Now I hate her."

Good Lord, the man sounded insane. Shivers crept over Cassi's back and tingled in her scalp. She flipped her hand through the mass of hair on the one side and took her time answering. "I'm sorry." What else could she say? She needed to get the lunatic out of here and first thing in the morning; she'd get her locks changed and an alarm system installed.

"I liked Raoul. Sometimes, he'd teach me boxing moves. I thought he was my friend."

"You took a beating because of him."

"They almost killed me. Dani was furious." In a sudden, unexpected way, he lurched to his feet. "I'll leave. I don't want to hurt you."

You could try! But my friend, in your stoned condition, the opposite would happen. Then again, insanity breeds strength. "Okay. And Juan...?"

He stopped on his way to the door. He didn't turn around. "Yeah?"

"Next time knock and wait till I open the door."

He chuckled. It wasn't a happy sound. It gave her the creeps.

He left and she rushed to lock up behind him. Then her knees gave out so she had to sit down again. What a strange, sad, scary man.

Why hadn't she asked him who had killed her brother? They'd touched on the subject. She thought back to his words and knew he'd threatened her when he'd said, "I don't want to hurt you." Except, if forced, he would. And being alone with him just now—well it wouldn't have been a smart time to anger the guy.

Instead, she decided to wait and maneuver a set-up at the club, like she had with Tommy Wilkens. One thing for certain, crazy Juan Acedo had to go to jail. After what he'd done to her brother, standing by and watching while another shot him, the dude couldn't be allowed to walk around free, even if he wasn't the shooter himself. He'd been there.

Chapter
Thirty-five

Cass waited throughout the early part of the day for Trace to appear and wasn't disappointed.

He showed up around lunch time just after the locksmith left and he looked haggard. She walked into his arms and he hugged her hard, wouldn't let her go, clung as if he needed her strength.

Knowing how much he suffered, she gladly let him draw solace, offering comfort from soft whispers, kisses and her arms.

"I'm not sorry she died, Trace. But I am so very sorry that she had cancer in the first place."

His voice drifted to her. "She loved you, Cassi. I knew it from the way she acted. Told me you needed careful handling and a gentle touch. Not to let you get away."

"She's right about not letting me get away. I'm right where I want to be."

Holding her close, he wouldn't allow her to see

his face and she had no doubts as to why. She'd felt him shudder and had heard the faint sounds of his grief. Why men seemed to think it weak to cry in front of a woman, she'd never know. The macho males in her family had been the same way. Yet rather than embarrass him, she just waited until he was ready to face her.

When he did, she could see the dampness; his spiky eyelashes clumped together, his Adam's apple wobbling as he swallowed to contain his emotion.

Often, his longish hair got a work-through. This morning it looked as if he'd pulled at it non-stop. In total disarray, his waves gave him a youthful appearance that she liked. Without a suit, wearing jeans and a short-sleeved turquoise cotton shirt, he hardly resembled Detective Trace Maguire at all.

"Can I make you lunch?"

"I can't stay that long, honey. There's too many things that need to be tied up. I just needed a hug. And to tell you that mom didn't want a big splash or a funeral. Didn't believe in drawing out the end like that. All she wanted was for me to spread her ashes over the desert at a picnic place we used to go to when I was a boy. When it's time, will you go with me?"

"Of course." She caressed his cheek and then hugged him hard, her arms around his waist. "Trace, I'm so sorry about her passing. Even though it was best for her, these last months were pure misery for you."

He tightened his hold on her. "I mean this with no disrespect, but I'm glad she's gone and her suffering has stopped. My only regret is that I wasn't there with her in the end."

Cassi nodded. "That, I can understand. I'd feel the same way. At least with Raoul, I was with him right after he died and if there's such a thing as a human spirit hovering around their body, then he knew it. When I thought about it later, it comforted me."

He sighed, his whole body shuddering. "Shit, Cassi, I'd have given anything to have been there with her. I'm just so glad she had Mary."

"Plus, we'd visited her earlier, and for that, we can be thankful."

"True." He drew her back, searching for her lips and gave her a kiss of such sweetness, that she felt the tears gather in her own eyes. Then he turned to leave and stopped at the doorway.

"Darlin', who was that pulling away as I drove up?"

Without planning her reply, she answered. "The locksmith."

He stiffened. "You got your locks replaced? Why?"

She took one of the keys off the counter and stepped forward to hand it to him. "I wanted to give you a key of your own rather than you having to use the hidden one. It seemed safer."

He searched her expression and his eyes narrowed. "That's the whole reason."

"Of course. You know it wasn't a good idea for you to be forced to get the hidden one every time you wanted to come in. People could see you replace it. They could have broken in, right? I just thought I was being prudent."

"You were. I'm proud of you for being careful." He reached for the key and while they both still held it, he hesitated. "Any other reasons I should know about?"

Thank you, Lord. He'd given her the out she needed. Shaking her head she answered him. "Nope. Before you leave, babe, I wanted to ask you one last thing. When we were at Mani's funeral yesterday, did her uncle have a nickname for her?" Not wanting to put words in his mouth, she'd left her question vague.

Trace rubbed the back of his neck his expression thoughtful. "As a matter of fact, he did. Called her Leni. Why?"

"No particular reason. I'm still shocked that she was related to Mani in any way. Another thing, I should mention that she has a tattoo on her back like the one the rest of the *Armas* gang wear. She'd had hers reworked with scrolls and flowers, yet if one knew what to look for, it was pretty clear."

Trace's interest peaked. "How do you know?"

"Saw it in the dressing room at the gym. She covers it up with her tops."

"So, what're you saying? That she must have been a gang member at one time?"

"Looks that way to me."

"I'll check into it." Smiling, he leaned over for a final kiss, stuck his key in his pocket and left.

Chapter
Thirty-six

Later, at the gym, while Rusty and Arlene both sat transfixed, Cassi watched the videos of Arlene's last fight with them. She'd gotten over her anger at Arlene. Something Trace had told her about Arlene's reaction to finding out that Raoul was her brother made her wonder if Arlene knew of their relationship. She'd decided to give her the benefit of the doubt, mainly for Rusty's sake.

Her musing interrupted, she listened to their banter. "It's about time you moved into this century, old man." Arlene pointed at the video camera and then glared at him. "I've been telling you it was a necessary tool. Now I can see where I should concentrate my efforts. Like whether I drop the shoulder you keep yelling at me about."

"Yeah, yeah! What? You think money grows on trees around here? There's a lot of expenses in running a class joint like Rusty's."

"Aw, give me a break. You're just a cheap son of a bitch and we both know it." The teasing note in her voice made her remarks acceptable and Cass didn't bristle like she had numerous times when they'd been serious.

While the other two sparred insults, a thought niggled yet remained elusive. What memory was riding her back, pinching and pulling to be recollected? She wished it would come to her because deep down, she sensed its importance.

"Hey, Cass, you with us?"

Arlene answered Rusty before Cassi had the chance. "Her head's in the clouds as usual."

Rusty eyeballed her and grinned. "Can't be that bad. Beats you often enough, doesn't she?"

Surprised that the other girl didn't bristle and stomp away, Cass winked at Arlene with a friendly grin and settled into paying attention. Moving on, they discussed the various ways her opponent had managed to get past Arlene and how she could have retaliated with more success.

Pumped from watching, not just her errors but the ways she'd excelled, Arlene said. "Cass you want to go a few rounds so we can practice these moves?"

"Sure Leni. Give me a few minutes to change."

Watching for a reaction, she wasn't disappointed. Arlene's face hardened and she showed attitude. Before she could say anything, Rusty stood up between them. "Get going, brats. I have a lot to do this morning. I don't have all day to mess around with you two."

In the dressing room, she kept rethinking their earlier discussion. Whatever niggled to get through just hovered enough to piss her off.

Blasted hell! There's something I need to remember?

Once in the ring, Arlene came after her with way more sass than was called for. Pissed, Cass pushed her way out of an uncalled for clinch for the fifth time. Punched again in a sneak attack where Arlene hadn't broken according to the rules and then taking a right hook that wouldn't have been allowed, Cass had enough. Hearing Rusty's shout of disgust from the sidelines, she knew he was getting angry also.

Time to stop Arlene's foolishness...

If Arlene planned to pulverize her, Cassi had no intentions of making it easy for her to do so. Instead, she switched, using her Taekwondo moves from her brother's teachings of Gwon Gyokdo. It was a hybrid style that brought her legs and feet into play rather than just her fists.

Shoving Arlene off her yet again, skipping out of arms way, she used her foot to trip the other girl and they both went down. She grabbed Arlene's hand and with her own legs imprisoning the other's chest so she couldn't move, she trapped her in such a way that unless she wanted to break a bone, the fight had ended. Cass knew it and so did Arlene.

Confined now, spitting mad, she quit wriggling, gave up and lay still knowing Cass would release her.

Anger seething, Cass snarled so only the two of them could hear. "What the fuck's your problem?"

"Don't ever call me Leni again."

Ahhh....

Chapter
Thirty-seven

Sam grinned when he saw her approach later. "Hey, princess. You're looking rather spiffy tonight."

Cass had gotten her hair redone, sprayed the short side pink to match the rhinestone danglers that tickled her shoulders and bought a new pair of boots with higher heels than she normally wore. After leaving the gym, still smarting from the beating Arlene had tried to lay on her, she'd decided a treat was in store.

First, she'd taken her new bike out into the hills and spun it wide open. Working the gears, brakes and gas, leaning into the corners, she found her rhythm and relaxed into the ride. Flying along the empty highway, weaving, speeding, freedom so sweet she could taste it, she felt renewed, one with the universe.

The asphalt from the road and the red earthy

sand around her imparted its absorbed heat. The various desert smells of dried grasses and dust assaulted her as well. Never before had she experienced the sensations of power her outing yielded. As a rider, this rush didn't come close to that of the driver whose hands were on the controls and who made the ultimate decisions.

Memories of her and Raoul surfaced and it was like she could feel him behind her, revelling in the sense of freedom riding had always brought with it. If she let her mind drift, his voice came clear, urging her on and laughing in the way he used to when they'd ride together.

Then she pictured her and Trace one day, riding on the same bike or each having their own. Hell, she'd never even asked him if he liked motorcycles. Smiling, full to bursting with the joy of being alive, she stuck that in her memory bank and decided she'd ask him the next time they were together.

Finally, filled to bursting, her emotional high leaving her reeling, she retraced her way home and ended at the salon where her new hairdresser, Lela, had set her up for an appointment. Next, she'd shopped at the shoe store two doors down and blew big bucks on the high-heeled yet comfortable boots she couldn't resist.

Later driving to work, the gloom set in. After her lovely afternoon, she hated like hell to come into this dump full of potheads, drunks and gang members with no futures ahead and besmirched pasts behind.

How many of these guys faced themselves in the mirror every morning without regrets? If any did, it wouldn't be done sober. And she was surrounded by these dudes every night. Hopefully, not for much longer.

The only part of the job she liked was working the bar with Sam. He made her feel safe in a place full of danger.

"Hey, Sammy." She teased. "Has it been very awful tonight?"

"Nope, *Cassidy*... Quite a few of the gang are still being detained at the jail, cooling their heels and likely pissed because of it. Dani's been like a rabid bitch with her snout full of porcupine quills, ranting and raving about Las Vegas's finest. I wouldn't mess with her if I were you. Not tonight."

"Yes daddy." She was in a playful mood after her day and poor Sam would suffer her *joie de vie*.

He shrugged. "Just so you know, baby doll. There're three things without a conscience: a stiff prick, a buck and Dani Andino. Got it?"

Laughing, she answered. "Okie-dokie! I'll stay out of her way." She winked and then started organizing the clean glasses, arranging them for easy reach and making sure the fridges were full of their most popular beer. As they worked together, she waited for her opportunity during a lull. "Question, Sam. Any chance you know one of the girls working upstairs, chick with long blonde hair?"

"You mean Faith? They call her Sunshine sometimes."

"Is she the only one that fits that description?"

"Yeah. There's a dark-haired bitch who fancies herself as Dani's favorite and a few others who come and go. Sunshine's been here for a long time I think. Shame, too, because the kid can't be more than eighteen."

"How do they get these girls to work in places like this, Sam? I know I'm naive and a bit of a prude but good Lord, who in their right mind wants to service creeps like the ones who hang out upstairs?"

"See, and there I thought you told me that the cops had picked you up for prostitution and that's how you knew that detective who came sniffing after you the first night you worked here." He moved in close. "What's up Cass?"

She leaned over so her hair covered the one side of her face and kept her expression bland. "I lied. He'd been on the case when Raoul got shot and had some questions. To stop any awkwardness, I didn't want to let everyone know I was Raoul's relative. Besides, you had me pegged right from the start, didn't you?"

"Ya think? It wasn't hard to see you had no clue. Though you do now so listen to my advice. Quit messing with stuff that could get you killed." He leaned in and lifted her hair to tuck it behind her ear. His voice gentled and his eyes shot tenderness. "Let the police handle the case, kid. As much as I'd hate for you to leave, I sure as hell don't want to see you hurt."

She put her hand over his still resting on her hair and squeezed. "No can do, bud. Not just yet. Soon, I think. Look, I have another lead on who might know about Raoul's murder. I need to question her and I kinda promised not to go back upstairs. So I need your help."

Sam's eyes froze over. "Jesus, Cass. Trace will kill me if I help you."

"He won't have to know. Please, Sam. I just found out that Sunshine and Raoul had a romance going and I think she might have some information. She's close to those crazies up there and we both know many of those losers blabber like schoolgirls when they're high."

"Hell, pal, even if she does have evidence, the girl's never sober. From what I've heard, she's been hitting the hard stuff and doesn't like to come down for long. So even if you get the opportunity to talk to her, chances are, she'll be useless."

"Could be you're right. But you have to understand. I've got to."

Suddenly, an empty can smacked the bar and Cassi looked up into the eyes of a furious customer.

Chapter
Thirty-eight

Cassi moved to serve the newcomer. "Hi, Juan. What can I get for you?"

"How come you let that dipshit fondle your face?"

Stunned, anger beginning low in a stomach that had clenched from the idiot's words, she reacted. "Seriously? You're questioning me about my boss?"

"He was touching you. I saw him."

"Did you hear what he said?"

"No—"

"Then fuck off, man. As my friend, he was trying to talk me into quitting my job because he's worried about me working in a shithole like this and hanging out with the likes of you."

Abashed, looking like a kid smacked by a mom teaching him manners, Juan held up his hands. "I didn't know. Sorry. I—"

Interrupting yet again, Cass drove home her point. "Look, man. Don't be a dick. I like you. We're friends. Okay? But I have other people I care about too... like you care about Mary. So you won't be making any brownie points with me if you mess around like this with your possessive bullshit."

"Sure. Okay." His wobbly smile worked hard to look sincere. "Can I have another beer? I'm on shift soon and I can't be late."

Cass got him his favorite and waved away his money. Making her voice easy, even soft, she nattered. "I understand Dani's in a snit after the warehouse got hit by the police the other night."

Happy again, Juan leaned in close. "It wasn't the police, Cass. It was the fucking FBI. They seized everything, even caught two of the guys who had outstanding warrants for armed robbery. Bloody good thing that Dani doesn't keep any of her private files or stuff that could link her to the place. You know, prove her involvement. The cops, they ransacked the joint and took all the product, arrested a few of the slackers. The rest of us made it out."

"You were there when it was hit?"

"Yeah. We have a back door no one knows about and a lot of us were able to escape."

"How cool is that?" She played along, seemingly impressed by his confidence.

"Won't she be afraid one of the guys arrested will talk, give evidence against her so they might get a lesser sentence?"

Juan's face showed his shock at her absurd remark. "Seriously, dude? Anyone blabs and they wouldn't last a day. She's got a long reach."

Laughing as if she had made a joke, she added. "I'm just fuckin' with you. I kinda knew that. Did you manage to save anything?"

"We didn't get out enough. There's orders to fill or the customers will jump ship. No one is faithful in this business, not unless they're terrified and most are. Scared or not, they still need their shit. Dani had to suckhole the old gang in L.A. to help her out. Let me tell you, she paid premium. I've never seen her this pissed since she dumped the old boss and cut him loose."

"The old boss?"

"He's the one who started this Vegas branch for the *Armas*, a nutcase and good riddance."

Not very interested in the olden days, Cass changed the topic. "Are you still working from the same warehouse?"

"After the police raided it? Not likely. She's moved us back here to the club, in the basement. I'm glad cause I'll be closer to you." He patted her hand but didn't leave his own on hers long enough for her to push him away.

Cass smiled and looked around at the lack of customers. The periodical drifters who came in, spent their money or played pool were obvious. As for the rest of the regular gang, there were very few.

"I'm glad it's slack in here tonight. Gives us a chance to bullshit. I wanted to ask you, Juan."

He heard the seriousness in her voice and stiffened. First, he rubbed at the black, coarse hair on his arm, so thick it could be a possible turnoff for anyone not of the animal kingdom. Then he nodded once. "What?"

"I know you were there the night my brother was shot."

His eyes narrowed and a cold expression wiped out his indulgence.

"I also know you tried to stop it and they gave you a beating for your trouble. What I need is for you to tell me who else was there."

"Are you kidding me?"

"I heard there was a girl involved." Thinking fast, Cass added a hook to see how it would pan out. "And she shot Raoul. I just wanted to know who."

Juan pushed away from the bar and dropped his empty can down, his expression sullen. "You want I should rat on a gang member?"

"Of course not. I'm not the police, Juan."

"Yet you're sleeping with a cop, ain'tcha?" His face mean now, he spit out his anger and stomped away. Darkened with disappointment, his eyes had shone pure hate for long enough to make her skin crawl.

With her heart now lodged in her throat, Cass realized she might have ruined any chance she ever had with the man. In fact, she'd just made a very bad enemy.

Shit!

Chapter
Thirty-nine

Trepidation set in and wouldn't be squashed. Juan was a sicko, a stalker who already gave Cass the creeps. Now she'd made him an enemy by her foolish questions.

Replaying every word she'd said, she had to accept that because of her inexperience, she'd actually put him at the scene of a murder and it had been Sergio Mendes who'd told her that he'd been there. No wonder he'd reacted.

Thinking back, she realized he hadn't seemed so upset at her knowing he'd been one of the three guys. No doubt—when she admitted she knew he'd been beaten for having disobeyed Dani's orders, she'd given him his alibi for not being the shooter.

Her mind swung this way and that and still came back to the same conclusion. Though Juan hadn't confirmed her theory, she trusted Sergio's theory of there being a female involved. In her semi-conscious recollections, all her instincts told her it had to be true.

Besides, Juan hadn't said there wasn't a woman there that night. All he'd fussed about was her wanting him to rat on a gang member.

Therefore, if it were true, just maybe, the bitch had shot Raoul.

"Cass, come back to earth, dude. You've got customers. There's one in the back who just arrived and wants special attention. Bring him a beer and then get rid of the idiot. He shouldn't be coming in here, it's dangerous for him. If Dani ever figures out he's one of the cops who raided her warehouse, there'd be hell to pay."

With her heart tripping to the tune of the music pounding on the loudspeaker, she snagged a cold bottle from the fridge and swaggered her way to the table at the back of the room.

With each step closer, her reactions accelerated so that by the time she slid into the chair across from him, she was breathless and full to bursting with gladness.

He waited for her to speak and so she did. "Sam's mad at you for coming here."

"And you?"

"I love seeing you any time, you know that." She reached her foot across to his and nudged his leg, loving that he reached down to catch her boot and bring it up to his lap.

He squeezed the soft leather and positioned her foot so she felt the bulge he didn't try to hide. For a few seconds, a tide of sensations overwhelmed, making her breasts tighten and her muscles pinch in delicate areas now wet from wanting.

Then she remembered the video cameras that Dani had ordered set up around the joint so she could watch for any spies from other gangs. They liked to come in and pick up talk. *Video cameras... that's it!*

Thankful for the darkness, she slid her foot away. "You look tired. Has it been very bad?"

Luminous with passion, his eyes gentled. "Just time-consuming. The paperwork for mom's cremation took most of the morning and then I had to go in to work and see if I could shake any of the prisoners we apprehended in the raid from the other night."

"No one talked, did they?" She reached to sip his beer, the smell having drawn her interest. Lately, she'd gotten a liking for the brew.

Looking sour, he answered, "Not surprising. We didn't expect anyone would, even with the incentives of a misdemeanor and less jail time. One of the perps was looking at a possible life sentence as a third-time felon and no way he'd swing. Though we gave it a go in case."

"Juan warned me that they wouldn't, said they were too afraid of the repercussions from Dani. I guess I believe him now."

"You talked to him?"

"Kind of." Shifting uncomfortably, Cass confessed. "I knew you'd be angry but I told him I had information that he'd been at the scene the night Raoul died."

Trace leaned forward. His eyes shot venom from under the ball cap pulled low. Gritty with anger, he growled, "You what? How the hell did you know he'd been there?"

Trying to look as innocent as possible, her eyes wide, she answered, "Sergio Mendes called and gave me the info. Said he knew of three people who had been at the shooting, Miguel, Tommy and Juan Acedo."

"Why the fuck didn't you tell me this earlier. We would have picked him up, had a little talk with him, forced him to reveal what he knew."

"He told me tonight he'd never rat on any gang members, in fact he got quite incensed that I'd bring it up and question him. And that was even after I told him I knew he hadn't been the shooter. In fact, I reminded him that I knew Dani had ordered him beaten for not pulling the trigger."

Stiff with resentment, he demanded an answer. "And you're only telling me this now." Trace crossed his arms, leaned back and glared. "Why?"

Wetting her dry mouth with another sip of the cold yeasty liquid, she admitted. "Because when I questioned him, he got scary-mean and... well..., he worries the shit out of me. With his stalking and—"

He spit out one word, "Stalking?" Eyes bulging, his whole body stiff with resentment, Cass had never seen Trace this angry before.

Talking fast, hoping to smooth troubled waters, she babbled, "Sometimes he'd stay outside the house at night, smoke joints and watch the place. Stupid, kid stuff, he never hurt me. Scared me when he broke in... "

Trace's head had dropped into his arms. His powerful shoulders seemed to be shaking and his whole demeanor made her nervous.

"Trace?"

Slowly his head lifted and though he wore a grin and still chuckled, there wasn't an ounce of humor in his face. "I can't *believe* you." Voice rising, his shirt tightened over clenched muscles and his face paled. "A librarian for Crissakes! I might add, one who's dating a cop! And she doesn't think to mention that some wack-job's stalking her, scaring the shit out of her and breaking into her house." He caught her eyes. Only hers flinched. "You never cease to amaze me, lady." He made as if to stand and she reached out to stop him.

"What are you going to do?"

"Arrest him."

"He's working here tonight. It's too dangerous for you to mess around out back by yourself. Promise me you'll wait until he's at home and you have backup."

Trace leaned over so his face stopped within inches of hers. "Promise me you won't talk to him again tonight and I'll organise some backup and wait until he comes off shift."

"I promise I won't seek him out. If he orders a beer, I'll let Sam look after him, okay?"

"Fine."

"One more thing... I just remembered something important, Trace."

His dark eyes softened. "Is it what you wanted to remember earlier?"

"Uh huh! You told me that the one regret you had was not being there when your mother passed. You also told me a while ago, after a lousy nurse had made you suspicious, you'd set up a camera so you could watch whatever went on with your mother. Was it still there in her room yesterday?"

"God, Cassi. I'd forgotten. And yes, I never did take it down after Mary came. I meant to but there was so much going on, it slipped my mind." His face aglow with delight, he added, "I'll check it out. Thanks baby."

Trace leaned forward and whispered. "If I'm real late visiting you tonight, will it matter?"

She grinned, relieved that he hadn't held onto his mad. "Not even a little. I'll be there, waiting..."

Chapter Forty

Trace had to get out of the club or he'd have done something foolish. Like haul the girl he adored out of that dive, kicking and screaming. Or smashed his way through the barriers, dragged Juan Acedo out by the scruff of his neck and beaten the shit out of the sick loser.

Just thinking about the shit Cassi had revealed made his flesh curdle.

Hands fisted and shoulders stiff, he hurried to the car so as not to do anything he'd regret. Sitting there, he crunched his neck from right to left, easing the tense muscles and then he called Diane, his partner, and got her working on gathering a team for later. No way he'd let this night pass without arresting that bastard. He needed him off the streets and on his turf so he could work on him, see if he'd break.

Next, he texted Sam to be extra vigilant with

Cassi. The shit she'd shared had changed the rules and she was in more danger than she could even imagine.

After his mother had remembered that Paul Andino, Dani's father, had been sent up for life, he'd gotten together with the others in his department to research Dani and they passed on their findings.

This chick was trouble with a capital K for killer. Her files showed a pitiful situation. A girl, whose father rotted in jail for his many indiscretions, including murder, wasn't the best possible influence. No wonder she'd gotten into a heap of trouble in her teens. It could also be said that her bad choices were a direct result of her mother's love to party being more important than her love for her kid.

According to most of the neighbors they'd interviewed, all Mommy Dearest had cared about was men first, then booze and then money. Dani came way down the line until she grew boobs and learned how to play the game.

Turns out, her mother made money peddling her unsullied kid for a while until Dani turned sixteen and got smarter than Mamá. She flew the coop, leaving her old lady with a broken arm and the latest John with stab wounds and a painful dick from the vicious kick she'd strategically placed after robbing them both.

Seems she'd struck out on her own after that.

Joined a gang in L.A. and wrangled her way into becoming the boss's girlfriend. To this day, they still didn't have any information on *that* sick son of a bitch. Other than knowing the guy had been a genius in setting up his growing operation and staying out of the limelight, he'd faded into the past.

Instead, seeing the Pitbull tendencies in his girlfriend, he'd put her in command and not long after, he'd disappeared from the scene. Whether that came about through choice, or he got ousted by his girl, no one was talking. Within days, Dani moved into the number one spot.

With her background, no wonder the lady was brutal and had street smarts up the wazoo. No heart and no hesitancy to inflict pain, she fit the mold like Cinderella's slipper. Who could blame her if she'd changed lifestyles, gave up the weaker sex and now preferred women?

In particular, the crazy-assed hellion wanted Cassi.

His Cassi.

Chapter
Forty-one

Cass felt better after Trace's visit. It might have been rotten of her to have divulged her secrets in a public place. Knowing he'd have to restrict his reactions with all the gang members around, had given her the confidence to confess.

Though she didn't wear a tattoo, many of the guys and their girls had come to look on her as a friend, one of them and let's face it; if anyone messed with one of their own, that idiot was toast.

Suddenly, Floss, one of the bar maids came to fetch her. "Sam wants you up front, Cass. Something's crawled up his ass so be careful." The girl gave her a hang-in-there grin and sauntered off to wait on the table that had just filled with a bunch of party animals looking for a good time.

Cass made her way behind the bar and pitched in to help with the rush. Sam caught her eye and mouthed that he needed to talk. She shook her head and ignored his gesture. A niggling feeling told her that the news wouldn't be to her liking and the longer she could put it off, the better.

Once they'd gotten the worst of the panic taken care of, she followed Sam's nod to the back and met him there.

"What's up?"

"I talked to Sunshine and she said she'd meet you in the bathroom at midnight. Look, I'm not too sure about this at all. I think you're stirring a big barrel of snakes with the biggest being the boss. She finds out you're snooping into her shit, she'll be pissed. You know the lady's been mooning over you and soon she'll make her move. Are you prepared?"

"We've already talked. She knows I'm not interested."

He questioned her with his hands on his hips and his attitude pissy as hell. "And that makes any difference? You don't think she just takes what she wants?"

Cass straightened her shoulders and a cold force filled her. "She can try."

"Oh, baby, trust me. She will." He glanced at his watch and added. "Look, I just saw blondie sneak downstairs and she's in the little girl's room. Make it quick. I'll cover for you. Just remember, I want to know what she tells you."

"Deal." Nonchalant, playing it cool, Cass strolled to the bathroom and once there, she hurried over to the blonde who wavered on her feet and couldn't hold her gaze.

"Thanks for coming, Faith?"

"Whaddya want, Cassi? I'm not supposed to be here. I'm an upstairs girl." Her words were slurred, her slinky dress wrinkled as if she'd had it removed a few times and her makeup was smeared.

"Yeah, well about that, anytime you want out, let me know and I'll bankroll you a place at the best rehab center in California." She watched as the girl's face crumpled and repeated her offer. "I mean that, Faith. Raoul would have wanted me to help you."

Faith wavered, unsteady on her feet. "He was special, my Ray. He loved me." Faith mumbled, her eyes not meeting Cass's.

"Yes, he was. That's why I can't let his murderer go unpunished. I have to find out the names of everyone at the warehouse that night. Can you help me?"

Hands covering her mouth, her eyes wide with fright, Faith's head shook first left then right and then again faster. "No... I—"

Unexpectedly, the door burst open, slamming against the wall, sounding like a gunshot. Two girls entered. Not strangers like Cass expected. It was Maddy, the slutty dark-haired girl from upstairs who pictured herself as Dani's favorite, partnered with Toby, one of the newer downstairs waitresses.

As soon as Cass understood they intended to

make trouble, her stomach dropped like a steel ball. She clenched her fingers a few times to relieve the stress and synced herself for the battle.

Toby took the trouble to twist the lock on the door, making sure they wouldn't be interrupted. Then she stood sentinel with her arms crossed and a smug grin on her face.

Besides the knife clutched in her antagonist's fist, her nasty expression didn't waver. This wasn't playtime.

Chapter
Forty-two

Trace knew he'd have a few hours to kill before it was safe to move in on Acedo. The arrest worried him, would probably get him into trouble with that prick, Hank Lester, Chief of Detectives.

Other than Cassi's word, he had no hard evidence that Acedo had been at the warehouse the night Santino got shot. Sergio Mendes might be a credible informant to her. In fact he didn't doubt his veracity. But the chances of him getting that jerkoff to divulge who passed on the intel might be likened to Mickie-D's letting Burger King in on their Big Mac special sauce. It ain't gonna happen.

What if he worked on Acedo, drove home that he had reliable information, would the asshole fold? After all, he had no priors other than youthful misdemeanors like breaking and entering, stealing cigarettes and a couple of marijuana possession offences, nothing big, typical teenage bullshit. He hoped the guy might scare easy.

He knew Mary Devin, Kathleen's nurse, was Juan's adopted mother. Could he use her to influence the idiot into divulging everything about that night? Since, according to Cassi, he wasn't the shooter, they could promise him a lesser charge if he helped the crown win their case against the true perpetrator, even witness protection.

Hell, if nothing else, at least he'd get the chance to warn the loser to stay away from Cassi or else. And, he'd drive that 'or else' in real hard so the son of a bitch wouldn't be under any illusions.

Thinking out his impending moves, the drive to his mother's house passed way too fast. Opening the door to the dark hallway, a sad loneliness enshrouded him, forcing him to sit for a few minutes before going into her room.

The faint odor of their spaghetti dinner still perfumed the air and his heart lightened at the memory of his mom's quick attachment to Cassi. They'd hit it off better than he'd expected. Not surprising—they had a lot in common.

Both were stubborn to a fault. Both were beautiful yet unaware of that fact and therefore didn't put on any false airs. And both were intelligent. A trait he'd always hoped to find in a woman who'd one day be his wife. Unfortunately, in Cassi's case, she was too smart for her own good.

The girl gave him nightmares and would continue to do so until they solved the mystery of her brother's murder. Thinking about that night, he realized he'd be one step closer once they arrested Acedo. That would account for all three perpetrators. Then she'd have to give up her witch hunt and accept that the case was closed.

Sighing, relief riding him so his step lightened and the weight on his shoulders dissipated a little, he made his way into the bedroom. Once there, he saw that Mary had been an angel right to the very end.

She'd taken the sheets and covers from the bed, emptied the tabletops from the huge variety of medication bottles and had aired the room so that lingering smell of Kathleen's sickness had been replaced with the scent of fresh air, no doubt from a window having been left opened most of the day.

Trace went over to his mother's night table and lifted the prominent picture frame placed there. He smiled, as he always did. Kathleen had wrapped her arms around his neck, catching him unawares and pulling him to her as she'd smooched his cheek. Lit up with the joy of loving each other, both were laughing so that anyone who took the time to look at the photo found themselves grinning too.

Returning it to its place of honor, Trace went over to the cabinet across from the bed, moved the stack of books aside and searched in the flower arrangement for the hidden clock camera he'd set there some time ago.

Glad that the machine held a huge file of video, he took the camera with him to the easy chair he'd always used while visiting Kathleen and stopped the recording. Then he went to the beginning and fast-forwarded it to the time when he and Cassi had visited with her.

He pushed play and watched as sweet Mary brushed his mother's hair, agreeing with Kathleen that it looked better for having been washed. She'd worked magic with a curling iron and comb and within a few strokes, his mother had curls. All the while, the two ladies conversed, Kathleen even giggling as they planned the evening ahead.

Fast-forwarding through the part where Mary helped his mother get undressed, he stopped to watch just after she'd been settled for the night. Peaceful now from the medications Mary had given her, she slept for a short while and then the pain came back. Harsh, horrible, debilitating, she whimpered, her head twisting from side to side.

He zeroed in on her to see that she wasn't awake but still under the drug's influence. Poor woman hadn't had a full night's sleep for many long tortuous months.

He saw Mary enter and give her another dose of her medication which after a short time settled her once again. Mary sat beside her until the dugs had taken affect. Strangely, she then kissed Kathleen's forehead as if saying good-bye. Then still holding her hand, Mary stepped to the side.

Without warning, another person came into sight. Though the light had been turned low, Trace had no problem making out who he was. When the intruder lifted a pillow and headed for the figure on the bed, Trace let out a hoarse yell, loud, heartbreaking... pitiful.

Chapter
Forty-three

Cass stepped in front of Faith only to be pushed aside by the suddenly alert blonde.

"What are you doing here, Maddy?" The feisty little chick stood her ground.

"One could ask you the same question, Skank. You're supposed to be upstairs making Dani money with those perky boobs. Instead I find you meeting the bartender in the ladies room, no doubt carrying on."

Cass couldn't believe the innuendo the other girl had implied. "We were only having a normal conversation like any two women who meet in a public washroom."

Maddy's sneering expression brought giggles from her sidekick. "Who're you kidding, think I was born yesterday? You followed her in here, I saw it from upstairs. First you hit on my woman and now you're after one of her girls. I'm telling you, bitch, I'm sick of you and you're sneaky ways—time you learned your lesson."

Maddy lunged, her knife out front and at the same time, Faith reached forward as if to stop her and got herself slashed for her trouble. Blood spurted, landing on Maddy's face and her revealing red silk top.

Stunned, whimpers escaping, Faith pulled her arm away, clutching it to her chest. "You cut me?"

"Shit! Now look what you've done, you dumb blonde bitch. You got blood all over my blouse. I'll teach you..."

Sickened by the display of cruelty, Cass kicked out, her new boot landing hard on Maddy's upper thigh. After completing the full circle, the other left its imprint on the side of the fool's head. She went down.

Toby, thinking her buddy needed help, rushed to join the battle, intending to overpower Cass from behind. Not taking any chances, Cass shifted to the side so Toby missed her target. Following up, Cass backhanded her and then pushed her so hard the girl flew through an open stall and ended up draped over a toilet.

Good! You deserved that.

Worried, Cass rushed over to see Faith's injury. Knowing they had to stench the flow, she grabbed handfuls of paper towels and applied pressure. The strong stench of metallic sweetness took her back to the last time she'd been near a wound, only then she'd been hugging a bloody corpse, her brother Raoul.

Busy, neither of them paid any attention to Maddy who'd risen from the floor, determination for revenge carved over her ugly expression.

Survival instinct worked in Cass's favor. So did Faith's horrified look that made her aware of danger. Intuitive to most moves, she shifted her weight and reeled to the side so that the downward arc of the knife missed cutting her. Unfortunately, Maddy's weight on her back drove Cass into Faith, knocking the blonde girl's head against the porcelain sink before she slumped to the floor.

Trained to react, Cass twisted her body and held off the knife's next downward thrust. She grabbed the hand that clutched the weapon and using it, she took them both down. Making sure she landed on top, she drove her elbow into the other's chest and chopped at Maddy's wrist, watching as the weapon, now free, skidded out of reach.

Reacting like any street fighter would, Maddy wound her arm around Cass's throat, her unbreakable hold cutting off Cass's air. Struggling, pulling from one side to the other, the pain caused her to feel lightheaded. No matter which way she turned, the vice just tightened.

Unable to reach her opponent, Cass had to come up with another technique to escape. She brought her boot up and slammed the heel into the other's leg. A yell of pain followed as Maddy released the pressure to let Cass twist away and roll to her feet, all in one smooth move.

Not as fast, Maddy took time to retrieve her fallen knife. Holding it in her hand, she swept it upwards, close to Cass who twisted out of the way at the last second. Watching for an opportunity to either grab Maddy's arm in a hold, making the knife useless or kick out with her feet, Cass circled her enemy.

Reddened where Cass's boot had made contact, Maddy face wore an evil grin. Now in her realm, she continued her futile jabs. Cass moved like a dancer, her stance ready, watchful... waiting.

In the distance, she heard pounding on the door and knew someone had complained to Sam that others were hogging the restroom. Yep! Sam's bellow broke through and interrupted Maddy's vitriol.

Goading her, getting into her head like they did in the ring, Cass spoke while skipping back and forth, her fists up and ready. "I'll give you one thing you upstairs slut. You sure have a filthy mouth."

"Quit playing little-miss-goody-goody with me, you fucker, you're worse than I am. Sure, I get paid to give the guys a good time. At least I'm honest about it. And I don't put the moves on someone else's girlfriend."

Shocked from the asinine stupidity of her opponent, Cass said, "What'll it take for me to make you understand... I don't *want* Dani. I have a boyfriend and he's plenty enough for me."

Maddy's sneer fell a little short this time, as if Cass's truth was beginning to make sense. Then she shook it off and prepared to come at her again. "Go figure, you might not want her, but that red-headed bitch has the hots for you."

This time she lunged and caught Cass with her back against the sink.

The blade of the knife cut her upper arm, not deep, yet it stung like a son of a bitch. Holding Maddy's wrist up with both hands, Cass used her knee to deter the other from her intention to mutilate. Only the other twisted from the worst of the hit and came back at her again.

Bending to the side, Cass caught the other's arm and brought her elbow down with enough force to do damage and then used the back of her closed fist against Maddy's face.

About this time Sam, having had enough with the nonsense of the door being locked, kicked it in and was in time to see Cass throw the last punch and put the other across the room so she slid down the wall.

Sam surveyed the scene; Maddy slumped against the wall, Faith crumpled in a small pool of blood and another chick draped over a toilet in the first of five stalls. He glared her way. "What the hell's going on in here?"

"A little misunderstanding. I think you'd better call an ambulance." Cass rushed over to kneel beside Faith. The girl's lax body worried her and so did the blood pouring from both her forehead and the cut on her arm.

Dani suddenly appeared behind Sam and shoved him aside; her short red hair spiked out around her head added emphasis to her reddened cheeks and filthy temper. "What the fuck is going on in here? Sam? Cass? And why the hell are three of my girls out cold in the ladies' room?"

Chapter Forty-four

Trace went straight to his office with the evidence he'd found. First, he needed to organise his team so they could make an arrest. Then, he wanted to file his film evidence through proper channels. The faster they could filter it and make it clearer the better. He'd have the technicians upload it and do their magic.

Shocked, Trace never expected to see Lester, his prick of a boss sitting in his office with the door open. He knew the other to be a workaholic but it was late, past midnight.

Their eyes met across the semi-dark room. "Maguire. My office. Now!"

"Shit!" The last thing Trace wanted was to have a session with that schmuck riding his ass, expecting him to bow and stroke him for every bit of bullshit that poured from his big mouth.

The guy was way past his prime. Though

experienced, he had no idea of what went on in today's world of technology and speedy internet. So many times, when he'd been called to headquarters for workshops and presentations put on to help the old-timers keep up with today's fast-paced, digital world, the old fart had pled overwork or sickness.

Trace had no doubt he was just biding his last few months to retirement and in the meantime intended to go out with his record in tact, his arrests higher than usual and his men in line. He'd been riding them for months now, close cases, catch the bad guys... make me look good.

"Hey, boss, what's up?"

"Nice to see you giving a shit about the job for a change, Detective. I'd begun to think of you as a nine-to-five rookie rather than a cop who wanted to get ahead."

"Yeah, well, with my mom sick, there were a lot of nights I had to leave and stay with her, had no choice. That's all changed now."

Hank Lester's expression softened long enough for him to add, "Sorry about her passing, Trace. She was a credit to the profession."

Should I let the old guy know what's up? Trace wobbled until he remembered he had a murder on his hands and a killer to catch. The time to play games had passed. As he started explaining, Lester cut him off.

He pointed to a stack of files on the side of the

messy desk. His eyes lost their compassion and his tone deepened. "You still playing around with this Santino case? How come you haven't found me a suspect yet?"

"Actually, that's why I'm in the office tonight. Do you have time to watch a video?"

"I was just on my way out. My wife's visiting her sister so I decided to come in when it was quiet and get caught up."

"I think you'll want to see this one, sir. The film shows my mother being killed."

Stunned and showing it, Lester jerked back in his chair, his lazy stance taking on a whole new arrogance. "The fuck you say?"

Trace held up the clock camera and waved it towards his chief. "It's all here on video. My mother didn't pass away in her sleep like I was told. She was smothered to death."

His veneer of superiority faded, coated with horror, Lester demanded, "What kind of wacko bastard would kill a poor defenceless, sick woman?"

"The kind whose own mother put him up to it."

Chapter Forty-five

"Sam, call 911 and then get this mess cleaned up. Cass, are you alright?"

"Yeah! Just a scratch on my arm. It's Faith who took the worst."

"Okay, then. Go upstairs and wait for me in my office." It didn't take long for Dani Andino to take charge and prove herself the boss.

Cass hesitated and Dani ground her next words so they left no doubt whether she meant them or not. "Go, Cass. I mean it. I'll look after this mess and see to Sunshine."

Sam moved in behind her, took her arm and forced her to her feet. When she glanced up, he drilled her with his silent warning. *Don't mess around, baby.* He didn't need to say the words; she got the message from his raised eyebrow and insistent nod. Seeing it would be stupid to argue, she did as she was told.

Moments later, in Dani's fancy office with the state of the art computer equipment and a desk empty of anything except a few pieces of paper, she used her cell phone to text Trace that she looked forward to their time together later.

Apprehension rode her hard. She wished herself anywhere other than this closed-in space where the stench of pot clung to every surface. And the bottles of booze and dirty glasses on the top of the modern file cabinets told their own story.

When Dani appeared, her face cold and expressionless, every muscle in Cass's body stiffened with misgivings. The saliva dried up making it difficult to speak. Instead, she let the other open the dialogue.

"What the hell am I going to do with you, Sugar? That cut on your arm bad?" Dani stood in front of Cass, her arms crossed as she lounged against the edge of her small, black metal desk.

"No. The bleeding's stopped now."

"Good, get Sam to fix you up before you leave here tonight." In slow motion, she slipped in behind Cass's chair.

Positive that she felt the other girl's hand stroke her hair, Cass braced herself. But Dani retreated so fast, she didn't have time to react or even speak.

"Maddy was one of my best girls. She likes the money, hates the men and the idea of raping their wallets always gave her an extra high."

Again in front leaning against the desk, Dani's

jeans fit so tight one might think they'd been glued on. A crazy thought entered Cass's head –wouldn't they cut off her circulation, make it impossible for her to move? Seems that wasn't the case. It took no effort at all for Dani to lift herself to the top of the desk and perch in front of Cass, acting all friendly.

Cass asked—what to her—rated first in importance. "Is Faith going to be alright? Maddy pushed me against her and she hit her head on the sink. That was after your favorite slut slashed her with her knife."

"So it's Maddy's knife. Funny thing, earlier, she told me it was yours. So did Toby."

Incensed, Cass growled. "I don't need a knife, Dani. You should know that by now."

"Figured they were bullshitting me. Maddy's already had a few runarounds with others where they ended up sliced and diced. Guess that bitch has used up all her brownie points around here. Toby too. And looks like Faith's off to the hospital. Which means, I'm short a couple of girls for working upstairs. The money's better than bartending, Cass, and for you, I'd be willing to up the cut. Interested?"

"Not in this lifetime."

"Hey, don't get pissed. The word was – the cops were checking up on you your first day here on the job because you'd been on the streets and they didn't like that you were working here now."

Cass tried to look uncaring, even bored. "Yeah,

well, what no one bothered to mention is that I hated it and swore I'd never let anyone near me again unless it was my choice. Not enough money in the world would get me to change my mind. Some men are pure animals. They don't care about anything besides their own good time."

"I know what you mean. Had to eat when I was a kid, slumming put food on the table and a little extra dessert up the nose, if you know what I mean."

Cass nodded. Not understanding how anyone could want to give over control of their body for any reason in the world, she didn't answer.

"So you hate men, animals you called them. That's interesting. Here I thought you insinuated you were straight, had no interest in women?"

Flipping her head to the side, using her swathe of hair to hide behind, she admitted. "It's true. I've never been gay. And... not *all* men are animals."

Moving with speed that Cass didn't expect, Dani grabbed the arms of Cass's chair and straddled her legs. Then she leaned toward Cass, her musky perfume billowing around them, strong and overt. Speaking in a throaty low voice, she whispered. "Wanna see for sure?" Her eyes delved into secret places, as if she knew what to look for and Cass had a hell of a time holding her riveting gaze.

Finally she wet her lips and watched Dani's eyes follow her every move. Swallowing, Cassi admitted, "I'm in love with a guy."

Dani laughed—a raspy, sexy sound. "So? What's that got to do with anything? I don't want your heart, baby. I just want to fuck your body." Laughing at the shock Cass couldn't hide; Dani leaned in and kissed her lips.

Flinching, pulling back and twisting her head to the side, Cass implored. "Dani, if anyone else took such liberties, I'd have them on their back with my boot on their throat. But it's you. So I'm making an allowance." Cass turned back and her look didn't waver, didn't flinch, the god's honest truth shone from her cold, blue eyes. "Don't ever do that again."

Before Dani could react, Sam knocked at the door and then burst in. "The cops are here, boss. You'd better come now."

Chapter
Forty-six

Dani stepped back and released Cass from her imprisonment. She stroked Cass's cheek and winked once, then turned to Sam.

"What's up?"

"Better deal with this yourself." Sam glared at Cass, questions obvious in his narrowed gaze. He swung his eyes to Dani, his voice mean. "It's beyond my pay grade."

Dani shrugged and gestured to the door, "Let's check it out." He turned first, leaving the women to follow. Sam's concern didn't suit the man she worked with every night. He was a pillar of "not giving a shit" about most things. This time he appeared rattled.

Dani went first and then Cass. With her thoughts on Sam who'd been agitated, she didn't pay attention to the goings-on below until halfway down the wrought-iron staircase. Then she noticed a variety of things at once.

First, the music had stopped and other than a low rumbling of discontent, the place was eerie from the unfamiliar silence.

Smoke hung in a cloud of disgusting stench. The results, watery eyes and a god-awful bad taste were the aspects of working at the club that she hated the most.

Next, with the lights turned up from their normal low-keyed illumination, she could see everyone in the place at once. A group had gathered, semi-circle facing the bar, yet forming a ring around the central figures.

Various policemen were strategically placed, all holding weapons pointed towards those same central figures.

Rodrigo appeared, a straggly-haired, leather-vested man full of tats and a wiry beard shadowed him. They both hung back and watched.

And last, her gaze swiveled to where Detective Trace Maguire stood in front of Juan Acedo, his badge prominent in the hand he held out.

What in the world...?

Juan leaned against the bar, drinking a beer as if rooted in place.

"What do you want, cop?"

"Juan Acedo, you're under arrest for the murder of Kathleen Maguire—"

"What the fuck are you talking about? I never killed nobody." Juan sounded like every other criminal arrested in public. He pushed his way towards Trace, threatening, furious... hating.

Diane, Trace's partner, stepped up and kept her gun directed at Juan while Trace retrieved an item from his pocket. He flung Juan around so his stomach hit the bar. Now Trace had access to his wrists for the handcuffs.

"You can tell that to the judge, Acedo. Don't figure he'll believe you since we have evidence that proves the opposite."

Dani slid into the scene and put her hand out to stop her people from reacting. The guy, who looked like a movie version of a Hell's Angel dude, moved in behind her. "Juan shut your mouth. Don't talk to anyone but our lawyer. Got it?" Her look demanded he respond and shrinking somewhat, he did. Hiding fear under a veneer of surliness, he nodded.

Dani swung back to Trace, her control back in place. Attitude lacking any respect, she ground out her words, "You know, you're beginning to piss me off, Detective."

"I live to please." Trace bowed his head and grinned. The lack of humor made the gesture as sarcastic as hell.

"You better have fucking iron-clad proof of his guilt, or we'll have him out in twenty-four hours."

"Oh we do. A video that shows him in the act."

Juan screamed, spittle flying from the sides of his mouth. "That's entrapment."

"No you idiot, it's just pure bullshit luck... on my part." Trace flung Juan toward the two cops waiting. Cass heard them reading Juan his rights as they dragged him from the building.

Cass saw Trace scanning the joint and knew the minute he'd seen her on the stairs. She made sure the wound on her arm wasn't visible or he'd react and she didn't want to push his buttons. Not now.

Gritting his teeth, she saw his cheek bones tense and his raised eyebrow question her location. Before he could move, ambulance attendants exited the ladies room, cutting through the crowd with Faith on the stretcher, unconscious.

Forgetting everything, Cass rushed down the rest of the stairs and slowed when Sam blocked her way. His hand grabbed the back of her belt, effectively stopping her forward momentum.

Trace stepped in front of the stretcher, his attitude questioning. "I heard there'd been a bar-fight. Didn't know women were involved. What the hell happened?" Trace's inquiring look scanned the people around him. No one answered.

One of the ambulance attendants filled him in. "Don't know. But this girl's in need of immediate medical attention, Maguire. Some crazy cut her and did a number on the side of her head. She's unconscious. The other two are a bit woozy. They'll survive. Must have been quite a fight though."

Trace moved aside while his gaze zeroed in on

Cass. She saw the minute he registered her guilty expression and he went from official to protective in just a few seconds.

"I want this place shut down. Now."

"You got a warrant?" Dani moved into his space, offensive as all hell.

"I can have one in an hour." Trace didn't step back. He wasn't one of her men.

"Fine, Cop. You go get it. Meanwhile, in an hour, the place will be closed."

Chapter
Forty-seven

Knowing it would be fruitless to get a warrant giving him access to search the whole club, Trace headed back to the office, hoping instead to get a chance at Juan before he lawyered up.

He went over everything in his mind that had happened earlier. And the most troubling aspect of the situation, one he couldn't shake loose was seeing Cassi descending the stairs from a place she'd promised him not to go.

From his car phone, he called Sam hoping he'd answer and help Trace understand. After three rings, just as he intended to hit cancel, he heard the other man's gruff voice. "Yeah?"

"You got a few minutes, man?"

"I'm in the stock room so make it snappy."

"What the hell happened there tonight, Sam? I've never seen a cluster fuck like this one."

"Beats me, Bro. Cass asked me to make

arrangements for her to talk to one of the upstairs' girls, Faith Whitely and I agreed to set it up. Otherwise, she said she'd promised you she wouldn't go upstairs, yet in this case, she'd have to break her word because she needed to question this chick."

"So you fixed it?"

"Figured it was the lesser of two evils. Hey, what was I to do? I didn't want to force her hand, so I agreed. We both know if I hadn't, she'd have found another way. Or just gone ahead and lied."

"Why the hell did she need to speak to this Faith? What was so important she'd break her word? Not that it isn't the first time. She's gotten to be quite a pro with the bullshit."

"Hey, man, cool it! It rides her when she's forced into these situations. We both know it, so quit being a prick. Anyway, I arranged for Faith to meet with her in the downstairs ladies around midnight. Then I got busy and didn't notice that Maddy and Toby had joined them. Seems Maddy had a particular problem with our girl. She thinks Cass's moving in on Dani, and at the moment, Maddy's her favorite."

"Crissakes, you telling me that Faith got the blow to her head in a fight with Cass against those other two?"

"It's complicated. Seems that Cass is responsible for most of the injuries, just not the knife wounds."

"What? Man, are you shitting me?"

"Your chick is one kick-ass lady, Trace. Why are you so surprised?"

With a definite sour taste in his mouth, Trace answered. "Beat's the hell outta me."

"So you know. She didn't start it."

"Yeah. She never does. Who was that ugly prick with Rodrigo? The one that stood guard behind Dani earlier."

"Name's Pete Bradford. Mean son of a bitch. You don't wanna mess with that dude, bro. He's got a rep for being heartless, cares about one thing only... his Harley. Has it all decked out, looks like a fucking disco ball in the sunlight."

"Where'd he come from?"

"Word is—he's from L.A., Dani's replacement for Mani Abel. She sent for him a while ago. It took time for him to clear everything up on the coast. This guy's a killing waiting to happen."

"Jesus, that's all we needed. Another hard-ass lowlife."

"Tell me about it..."

Chapter
Forty-eight

Later in the unadorned interview room at the precinct, Juan had nothing to say. No matter how hard Trace pushed, the other's mouth stayed closed and his expression didn't waver. Prowling in front of the table where one water bottle adorned the place where Juan sat, Trace explained about the video evidence.

That got him zilch. Juan's bored expression didn't waver.

He told Juan they'd arrested Mary Devin and he didn't change. Pure indifference.

Until Trace mentioned Cass.

"I hear you been stalking Cassidy Santino, Poser, breaking into her house, scaring her. What's up with that shit?"

Juan's expression darkened, his body began to shake and his fists tightened. "Yeah, well at least I didn't fuck her, man. Cass isn't scared of me.

And, she's too good for you, asshole."

"Surprise! Seems we agree on something after all."

Trace waited, hoping it would be the opening he'd been working for. A way into this man's mind, so he'd know what the hell the other was thinking.

His ploy worked. Juan spoke again. "She's my friend. I was protecting her."

"Against what?"

"Against Sergio Mandalas, who else? Those *Soldados* put the word out that they would pay us back for the Mendes kill. They'd already gotten a hold of a few of our chicks, girlfriends of some of the men. They messed with them. No way I'd let them take Cassi. Her brother was my friend too."

"Yet you killed him."

Juan shot out of his chair, the chains from the handcuffs keeping him from getting at Trace. He slammed his fists down hard. "No fucking way, man. I tried to stop them. They beat me after I went against orders."

"You're full of shit, Acedo. Word is you were the shooter—"

Before Juan could retaliate, Diane opened the door and a high-priced, well-known, scumbag lawyer entered. "My client won't say another word, Detective. And I'm surprised at you're harassment, considering this innocent man's situation."

Trace almost didn't contain his frustration. His first inclination was to punch the slick prick in his well-groomed, clean-shaven face. Knowing the high-priced attorney would have had him up on assault charges stopped Trace from giving in to his craving.

That and his partner's hand on his arm and her whispered warning, "down boy" brought him to his senses.

The timely interruption wouldn't have pissed him off as much if Acedo's guilt hadn't appeared before he'd lowered his face. His flushed cheeks, along with the sweaty skin and the slippery way his eyes wavered gave away his secret.

All his years of training, dealing with the scum of Las Vegas, warned Trace that not only was the man a liar, he wasn't very good at it. Now they needed evidence. Find the weapon, a witness, anything that they could use in a court of law to convict this son of a bitch and give Cassi some closure.

Before he closed the door, Juan let loose a litany of swearing. Over the voice of his lawyer telling him to shut up, he added. "You want Santino's killer? Look for the chick. She's your killer, man. Not me."

Chapter
Forty-nine

Following orders from Dani and then Rodrigo, who'd stayed in the background keeping a low profile during the altercation, Cass hurried to start closing down.

As soon as the cops left, Dani gathered Pete Bradford and most of her men and disappeared below. It made Cass wonder if Trace's appearance and threats hadn't scared her into shutting down operations for the time being.

Having a place she needed to be, Cass rushed around, helping Floss clean tables. After they finished, she took over cashing out while Sam headed for the stock room to fill in the requisitions for their next day's order.

"Cass get in here." Sam stepped into the open, his cellphone disappearing into his back pocket.

"What, Sam? I need to finish this."

"Not until I fix your arm."

Having forgotten about her wound after all the excitement, she looked down and saw the bleeding had stopped on its own. "Its fine, Sam."

"No, chickie, it isn't. It needs to be cleaned and dressed. Get your ass in here."

Rather than argue, Cass went and sat on the stool he waved to, her body still tense from the earlier excitement. He peeled the foil packaging from the cleansing packet and cleaned the area well and then used the special bandages that would close the wound so it would heal without stitches.

"You're lucky she didn't cut you deeper."

"Too bad she cut me at all. I couldn't get out of her way in time. She's fast."

"No doubt! It's well known that she has a preference for her knife. And she's a vindictive little bitch so watch your back."

"She'll be gone according to Dani."

He gave her a don't-be-so-stupid look and changed the subject. "You gonna tell me what happened in there tonight?"

"It was pure spiteful jealousy on Maddy's part. She thinks I'm moving in on her ahhh... territory."

"Dani?"

"Yeah! I told her she was wrong. Seems she needed convincing."

"And you were just the girl to do that."

"Except Faith took my punishment, Sam. I need to get out of here so I can go and see if she's okay."

"You think that's a good idea? You never even

knew the kid."

"Yeah, well it turns out that Raoul and Faith had a thing going. I feel I kinda owe it to him to help her any way I can."

"Hey, I never knew that. Not surprising though since they both worked upstairs. How'd you find out?"

"Rusty, our trainer at the gym, said my brother had shown him a picture of a young, blonde chick with long curly hair. He'd told Rusty that she earned her living in a way that Rus wouldn't approve. Kinda figured she fit the description. When I confronted her tonight, she admitted they'd been involved."

Sam shook his head; sadness replacing his usual indifferent expression. "Jesus. They never stood a chance. That's tough, Sugar. I'm sorry."

"Yeah, me too. I wanted to talk to her and see if she had any idea who'd been at the crime scene the night Raoul was shot. After all, she had to have heard something. Men talk. Right?"

"Well, sure. We're blabbermouths given the right incentive. But these losers are terrified of the boss, Cass. You gotta understand that. They're hardened criminals not willing to take chances with their own balls, if you get my meaning."

Nodding, even grinning slightly because she knew Sam wanted to shock her into getting his message, she agreed, "I know who we're dealing with, Sam. Remember me? I also serve these foul-mouthed idiots night after night. Some are, as you say, hardened criminals, but many are just young druggies; wanting to live up to their bros in the gang and they don't think about their balls. These particular wannabies are just a whole lot of bullshit and posturing."

Sam scratched his two-day beard and chuckled. "You got me there, princess. About Juan..."

"What about Juan?" Cass had tried not to think about him or Trace's expression when he'd announced he was arresting Juan for the murder of his mother. She'd heard the crowd's gasp but it had been trivial compared to the shock that had blazed through her smugness.

Sorrow had pierced her armor at the thought that it had been her suggestion for Trace to bring Mary Delvin and therefore Juan Acedo into their lives. The sickening knowledge had dug at her, the worry ramped up at the thought he might blame her as much as she blamed herself.

She'd thought Mary had been perfect as a nurse, had seen the two women together and decided they had formed close ties and a warm friendship. My God, how could she have been so wrong?

Chapter Fifty

Once Cass explained to the nurses that she was Faith's stepsister, they let her into the room. Talk about being able to bullshit with a straight face. The harridan at the front desk had told her in no uncertain terms that they wouldn't allow anyone except family into Faith's room and she'd get no information about the girl's condition either.

Therefore, she created a link and snuck into the elevator, going to the floor where they gave her the room number and let her in to see Faith.

Just in time to catch the doctor on night duty, Cass lit into him. "How come my sister is still unconscious? Is that normal after a blow on the head? I would have thought you'd want her alert to be able to assess her condition."

"When she first arrived, we did some x-rays and tests. There's no immediate danger. She regained consciousness for a while and we'll be waking her periodically during the night to make sure she's lucid."

"I'm awake now." Faith's feeble voice had them both turning toward the bed. Cass let the doctor move in front of her so she could make gestures, pointing at herself and mouthing the word sister.

The slight nod told Cass the other girl understood and she settled down.

The young man, haggard from too many hours on shift, his stethoscope hanging at an angle, talked in a soothing way. "We have some results from the tests you underwent earlier, Miss Whitely. If you'd rather me give you them in private, I can have your sister leave."

Faith shook her head and her hand reached for Cass's. Together, they waited for the doc to scroll through pages on his tablet until he found the one he needed.

"Okay then. I have to tell you that we've been forced to administer special medications because of the methamphetamines in your system."

Faith stiffened; embarrassment unmistakable in her expression. "You know about that?"

"Yes, of course. Look, it's better to wean you off the drugs. Because of your miscarriage, we need to watch your blood levels. You're also malnourished, which is another worry—"

"Miscarriage?" Faith jerked upright and her weakness forced her to slump over the side. Both Cass and the doctor shot forward to straighten her so she wouldn't slip off the bed. "I've never been pregnant. The men have to wear condoms. It's the rule." Suddenly, she lost all color. "Oh!"

"What? Faith, what is it?"

Faith swiveled to Cass, her distress obvious. "The baby would have been Raoul's. He was the only man I've been with who didn't use protection." Tears streamed down her face as she looked first at Cass and then the doctor. "How long had I been pregnant for?"

"I'd say you would have just started the second trimester, possibly twelve to thirteen weeks. The fetus was tiny but then you haven't taken care of yourself, have you?"

"I swear, I didn't know I was pregnant." The distraught girl looked first at her doctor and then she turned to Cassi. "I had no idea. After Raoul died, I was so unhappy, I started taking heavy drugs, meth and shit like that. Oh my God, Cassi. If I'd have known there was a baby, I'd never have gone there. Please believe me. Up till then, I'd used marijuana and alcohol and that's it. After I lost Raoul, it seemed like I had nothing to live for." She drew in a large sobbing breath and the resulting heartbreaking wail made the resentment that had hit Cass falter and then dissolve.

"Oh God, I killed Raoul's baby." Faith twisted into a fetal position, closed her eyes and withdrew. Weeping, inconsolable, she crawled back inside herself and shut them out.

The doctor led Cass from the room and then turned to her after the door closed. "Taking the drugs didn't cause her to lose the baby. Miss Whitely took quite a knock to her head and in the subsequent fall, she must have sustained an injury to her stomach. We'll keep a close watch on her for the foreseeable future."

Guilt-ridden, thinking Faith would never have been in that ladies' room if not for her interference, Cass replied, "Thank you, Doctor. I think you'd better. I've never seen a more unhappy soul."

He nodded, glanced down at the tablet and switched screens. "I understand this girl worked at the Lipstick Club. Was she prostituting?"

Defensive, Cass bristled. "Does it matter?"

"Actually, yes it does. I've seen this over and over again and it's a quandary. Many are forced into prostitution because of experiences in their earlier years. So they turn to drugs to survive, giving up on any chance at an ordinary life and the drugs help them continue living their miserable existence. It's a vicious circle they can't seem to break."

"I don't judge, Doctor. At the same time, I don't understand it either."

"If you worked here and witnessed what we get to see every night, you wouldn't have that luxury of disinterest. You have to admit that Faith's lifestyle wasn't conducive to motherhood or being able to bear a healthy, normal child. Meth babies are a sad outcome of the choices these women make."

As remorseful as Cass felt to agree, she had to. "That breaks my heart. We lost Raoul a while ago and having his baby would have taken away a lot of the anger and heartbreak over his death."

Nodding, the doc reached out to pat her hand. "Then this whole debacle is a shame."

Unable to stop her wobbling chin, or the flooding agony, she turned from him to make her way out of the building. Rivers of tears blurred the dark, hot night.

Blinking, stumbling, she made her way to her car where she finally broke down and released the massive ball of pain that had made breathing so difficult. Wrapping her arms around her midriff, she swayed back and forth.

God, Raoul... I'm so sorry.

Chapter
Fifty-one

What seemed like a lifetime later, Trace pulled up in front of Cassi's and noticed her car was missing. The house looked dark and locked up tight. At first, he'd vacillated about whether he could be with her that night, so much had happened.

In the end, he'd decided he had no choice. The huge need building in his belly to see her, hug the woman, give her shit and then love the dickens out of the beautiful brat couldn't be ignored.

Now it looked as if she'd turned the tables on him by not being there waiting. Worry swelled and overtook his calm. Where the hell *was* she? It was past two a.m. Trace knew by what Sam had said earlier that they were given orders to close the joint. So Cassi would have left well over an hour ago.

Fear clawed at his earlier smugness. Thinking he had the right to decide if they would be together that night, he hadn't even taken into consideration whether or not Cassi would be available. Teach him right for taking her for granted and thinking that his role in this relationship gave him the power.

Stupid jerk! She has a life too.

His mother had taught him better. Cassi was his equal not his underling and he'd better not forget that with this girl. From the beginning of their connection, she'd wavered, leaning on him and letting him tell her what to do. As time passed though, more and more, she'd taken hold of the reins and made her own decisions. Hadn't they almost lost each other after the episode with Tommy Wilkens?

She's disobeyed his orders. And he'd fought hard to overcome the shock that the woman had a mind of her own. He'd stayed away for as long as he could. But in the end, she'd lured him back to her with her beautiful heart, luscious body and exciting temperament. The mix of loving woman, obedient sex slave and fiery female had been too much. How could any man stay away from that?

A knock at his window pulled him out of his slumbering daze. Shocked that he'd not seen her car arrive, he opened the door, stepped out into the night and caught the trembling body that flung itself into his arms.

***

Cass couldn't believe her luck when she saw

Trace slouched in his front seat. Why hadn't he used his key and gone into the house to wait? She didn't know but it didn't matter. As long as he was here. Tonight of all nights, she needed him.

"Love, I'm so glad you came over. I wasn't sure if you would."

"Why wouldn't I? Because you disobeyed my explicit orders and went upstairs at the club where Sam couldn't protect you? Or because you were in a chick brawl? Or maybe because you lied to me? If those aren't enough reasons to stay away, I'm sure I can come up with more."

The shock still lingering in his eyes stopped her from reacting. That and when he followed up his diatribe, he added a phrase that made his behavior acceptable.

"Fuck me, I'm sorry, Cassidy. I think I took a stupid pill when you weren't here. You drive me crazy, woman. I don't know how to handle you."

That's when he ruined it.

"Handle me? Like I'm a stupid dog who needs to be trained?" Fire shot out of her mouth straight from the buildup of acid in her stomach. If he wanted a fight, she'd give him one.

"Shut up out there you two. People are trying to sleep."

Trace turned to the house across the way and saw the semi-naked man at the front door, his gleaming white underwear kept him from being obscene.

"Yeah, sorry, man. We'll take it inside." Trace put his arm around Cassi's waist and steered her in the direction of her front door.

"I'm a jerk, Cassi. Let's go talk like two educated adults. We'll figure it out."

Still a little miffed, Cass nodded and headed up the veranda stairs to the front entrance. She unlocked the bolt and disarmed the alarm next to the door by keying in the four digits.

Stunned, Trace stepped inside and as soon as she turned on the overhead light, he stopped in his tracks and pointed at the digital pad on the wall. "Since when did you have this installed?"

Sheepish, glad she'd already confessed earlier to having Juan break into her house, she admitted. "I took your advice. Or was it Rusty's?" Dithering, she pretended to be unsure before continuing. Seeing his eyes narrow, she backed up a step. "Okay, I admit it scared me a little when Juan broke in and I wasn't home. But when he used my spare key and entered while I was in bed, I decided I'd had enough with all the surprise visitors. So I ordered this system." He continued to stare at her and she could see his mind at work. "I thought you'd be pleased."

"What do you mean... *all* the visitors?" His face darkened and she noticed that he'd clenched his hands.

Thinking fast on her feet, Cass added, "Sergio Mandalas first, then Billy and finally Juan. How many shocks does a girl need before she smartens up?"

"In most cases, I'd say one. In your case, I'd say multiple. Who's Billy?"

Bust-ted!

Chapter
Fifty-two

Cassi dropped her bag and kicked off her boots. "Right, you don't know about Billy Duran. He's a childhood friend of mine and Raoul's. We grew up together in the neighborhood. Since his family was dysfunctional, to say the least, Papa encouraged Billy to come and stay here as often as he wanted."

"You've never mentioned him before." Trace eased into a relaxed stance.

"It just never came up. Plus, I didn't know where he'd disappeared to. Then one night, after he heard about Raoul, he came here thinking to take care of me. Turns out, it was Billy who needed the help." She couldn't fake the soft tone in her voice and saw Trace react to her gentleness. "In the early days, he'd been like another brother to me and Raoul, Trace. I can't help caring about what happens to him. We set him up in California at a rehab clinic."

Cass revisited the night she'd come home to find

her friend in dire need of assistance. He'd been a mess, struggling to kick his drug habit on his own and she'd stepped in to take over, made arrangements with Rusty to see that Billy got the help he needed.

"We who?"

His sharp tone irritated the hell out of her. "Quit interrogating me."

"Sorry. Who helped you get Billy into a rehab facility?"

"If you have to know, it was Rusty who made it happen. He knew him also, though not as well as we did. Don't you see, him being an old friend, I had to do what I could."

"Of course you did." Trace relaxed his tetchy mood and reached out to gather her close. "Of course you did," he repeated. "Most others would have kicked him out and locked the door. Funny thing, I have no doubt you let him in and took care of the poor son of a bitch."

She nestled in close, wrapping her arms around his waist. "He wasn't always a misfit. At one time, Billy Duran was a top-notch lawyer who earned a lot of respect."

Trace stiffened in her arms. He seemed to hesitate, but after she pressed her body against his, he relaxed. "Let's not focus on other people anymore. I need you, Cassi. Come with me." He picked her up so she could wrap her legs around his waist and then began heading for the bedroom.

Once there, he tried peeling her clothes off, but she pushed his hands away, led him to the side of the bed and patted the seat next to her. "We need to talk."

Sliding his hands under her bottom, he picked her up so she perched on his lap and he nuzzled her neck. "No we don't."

With a twist of her face to the side, she allowed him greater access. Her voice huskier than usual, she insisted, "Yes, Trace, we do." She kissed him fiercely and then tore herself backward so he could see her expression. "You need to tell me about Kathleen and I need to tell you how very sorry I am to be the cause of so much grief."

Chapter Fifty-three

Stunned, he took her face in both his hands and stared into her eyes. Horrified, he saw tears well and knew when she bit her wobbly lip, he had a full-fledged situation on his hands. One that scared the bejesus out of him.

He didn't do tears well. Hell, the only time he'd ever seen his mother cry was when he'd reacted badly to her news about the cancer. His ranting and fear had been more than she could handle on top of her own. Her subsequent breakdown had him backing off so fast he'd left skid marks on the rug.

Smartening up, he'd pretended to be strong. Once he'd calmed her down and she rested, he'd headed over to his own place and cried like a baby for one hell of a long time.

He heard the sniff Cassi let loose and gave all his attention to stopping the deluge before it began.

"Honey, what are you saying? How can it be your fault that Juan killed her? If you hadn't reminded me to check the video, I might never have thought of it. Mary had already started tidying the bedroom and I had intentions of hiring her to clean everything out, all moms' personal clothes and belongings. She'd have added the clock into the thrift shop boxes and the evidence could have gone missing."

"Love, you wouldn't have hired Mary in the first place if I hadn't met Juan and told you about her."

Trace lay back on the bed and brought her along with him. Hands gentle, he caressed her cheek and then kissed her, keeping his hunger under control. She needed his understanding right now not his passion. The stroking pressure on her arm seemed to help as well as the butterfly kisses he scattered all over her face.

Her woeful expression dug its way into a hidden area in his heart that he'd always kept concealed, closed to all but his mom. It opened just enough for her to slide right in. His to love, protect – cherish.

Gathering her tighter to his body, he whispered words he knew to be true. "Darlin' listen to me. Mom was never going to get better. You do understand that, right?"

She sniffed again and nodded, her soft hair brushing against his chin.

"You know her suffering was like a nightmare for

me; watching the cancer torture her beyond belief. Even though the doctors warned us to be prepared, neither of us understood the ramifications. Just before she died, she admitted to Mary, who told me, that she wished she'd have gone along with my suggestion to pursue assisted suicide. When I'd first mentioned it, she'd refused, said it went against her beliefs, said she was strong and could take anything the good Lord dished out. Neither of us knew then that her system wouldn't tolerate the most effective medications."

"Oh, Trace, your poor mother. I respected her before I knew this. Now I'm filled with admiration. In her case, and I'm sure in others, death can be a blessing sometimes."

He nodded, tucked her head under his chin to hide his face. "The shock from the video has worn off somewhat. Just so you understand, when he put the pillow over her face, Mary had made sure she was already into a drugged sleep. It took a few seconds and her struggles were over. Crazy though it sounds, Mary stood by holding her hand and crying through the whole thing."

"Mary knew?"

"Of course. Who do you think set it up? Turns out, very few of her patients have lasted for long after Mary Devin is hired to look after them. I don't know whether that woman has invisible wings or horns, I truly don't."

"Me either." Cassi leaned over him and wiped

the tears he wasn't aware had slipped out to make their way to her forehead. She kissed the dampened skin, her soothing affection the perfect comfort to a man still in denial.

Nestling closer, her body half lying on top of his, she added, "So what happens now?"

"They picked Mary up earlier and brought her in. She'll need a good attorney but I, for one, will have trouble testifying against the woman. When you first told me about her, I checked her credentials and called a few of her previous families for references. They all spoke very highly of her skills and each family mentioned her sympathetic personality. They raved about her kindness and how she'd go the extra mile every time to see her patients had the best of care."

"I couldn't help noticing that your mother liked her—a lot."

"She loved her. From the day Mary arrived, I could see Mom was happier and in a much better place. Makes me think others will feel as I do. Is she the angel of mercy or the devil of death? I have no doubt that only her Maker can answer that with any certainty."

"But they'll have no trouble convicting Juan, will they?"

His voice hardened. Unable to share what Juan had revealed about the night Cassi's brother died, he answered without the respect he'd shown for Mary.

"Yeah, he'll go down. I have a feeling she's used him many times to do what she couldn't."

Chapter Fifty-four

Sensing Trace's exhaustion, Cassi prodded him to sit up so she could help him undress. Her guy had suffered so much in the last twenty-four hours that it was a privilege for her to care for him. That he'd let her—made her love him all the more.

He accepted her ministrations, her tenderness coaxing him into lying on his stomach with his head propped on his arms while she massaged his back. At first, his skin shivered from her touch but soon the kneading soothed.

She straddled him and let her rhythmic strokes drift over the powerful muscles the man had built over the years of taking care of his body. When she sensed his breathing had evened out, she slipped a cover over both of them and crawled in next to his side. Her arm wrapped around his waist so, for once, she held him while he drifted instead of the other way around.

Close to sleep, he lay quiet for a few moments and then it was as if a bolt of some rambling thought hit him. He jerked up on his elbow to look down on her.

Not comfortable with this position, Cass tried to squirm away. He stopped her with his leg over hers and his arm braced on the bed behind her.

"Oh no you don't, babe. You have some explaining to do. Best get it over with so we can put it behind us."

So close!

She huffed her exasperation, tucked the blanket over her naked breasts and lay flat rather than cuddling as before. "I thought you were asleep."

"Not quite. My brain's too full of questions."

"What do you want to know?"

"Why were you in a cat fight in the ladies room? A brawl, I might add, where one girl ended up in the hospital with knife wounds, concussed and out for the count while two others were laid flat from your attack?"

Put that way, Cass couldn't help seeing things from his point of view. She had some explaining to do.

First she tried to gather her thoughts, what she'd already shared and the secrets she'd kept. Then she traversed with care. Say as little as possible had become her motto. She hadn't forgotten his warning that she could be arrested for interfering with an ongoing murder investigation. "Faith

Whitely, the blonde girl known as Sunshine who was sent to the hospital, works upstairs and it turns out that Raoul had a relationship with her."

"He did? We asked about his relationships and got nowhere. How did you find out?"

"Rusty happened to mention that Raoul had once shown him a photo of a girl he cared about. Told Rus they worked together and then admitted she wouldn't be the kind of girl one would bring home to the family."

"Okay. What made you link Rusty's account of Raoul's girl to Faith?"

"Rusty said she had long blonde hair to her waist. The first time I went upstairs, I'd seen a girl on the dance floor who fit that description."

"And..."

"And I put the two pieces together."

After a few seconds, Trace spoke, his voice now droll, as if he knew her ploy and would play along. "They were hooked up?"

"Yes, I believe so."

"So you wanted to talk with her."

"Yes. I asked Sam to set it up. My promise to you, not to go upstairs, stopped me from just going to see her. Instead, I asked Sam to make the arrangements."

"Right. You planned to meet in the bathroom downstairs."

"Yes."

"Oh-kay?"

"I had the right girl. Faith told me they were in love."

"I can understand you wanting to talk with her but what was so important that you couldn't wait until the next day? Instead, you had him arrange it at midnight at the bar? That's what doesn't make any sense."

Shit! He wasn't going to cut her any slack.

"You know why."

"To question her about Raoul's murder."

She nodded.

"Excuse me?"

"Yes!" She slid as far away from him as she could without dislodging his hand or dropping over the edge. "Are you satisfied now?"

"Not even close."

"What else do you want to know?"

"What happened in the bathroom so they had to call an ambulance? And why do you have a bandage on your arm?"

"You noticed."

"Honey, I might be blind-sided by your beauty. That doesn't mean I don't see everything else."

Cass heard his sarcastic quip and relaxed. He'd calmed down and seemed more reasonable. She could deal with this Trace. On the other hand, he had a way of luring her into disclosing things she'd never intended to say. *Be careful!*

"One of the upstairs girls, Maddy, took exception to Dani treating me... well, being easy on me. She's jealous and decided to teach me a lesson. When she saw Faith sneak downstairs, she followed and brought a sidekick, one of the new waitresses from the bar."

"Did you get any time to talk with Faith?"

"Just long enough to ask her about Raoul and find out she knew nothing about that night he died."

"What? Your voice changed." He forced eye contact and she couldn't ignore his searching question. "Tell me."

Thinking fast, Cass decided the truth was best. "After work, I went to the hospital to see her. It turns out that because of the fight, she'd had a miscarriage. Faith admitted the one man she'd been with who hadn't used protection was Raoul."

"God! Cassi. Darlin'. I'm so sorry."

Now it was her turn to shed tears for having lost out on such a precious possibility.

***

Trace softened his kisses to appease her sorrow. She accepted his comforts as what they were intended to be, his way of showing her he cared that she was unhappy.

Soon, she appeared to want more, need more. By moving against him suggestively and calling his name in a demanding whisper, she coaxed him to change from her tender caregiver to her lover.

His caresses became firmer, his hands creating their own brand of magic. Taking her breast to his mouth, he lathed it, paying special attention to the perky nipple that swelled from his ministrations.

He bit gently, then sucked and kissed until she cried out and it was time to pay attention to the other. Her urging whimpers persuaded and his hands drifted lower to find her incredibly wet, the kind of welcome he loved.

Accepting that they both were in need of love and not sex, he did everything in his power to show her how much he cared. His strokes were extra light and his lips giving and not demanding. With every move of his body, every plunge and withdrawal, he whispered words that had grown in his heart and had never been uttered before. "I adore you, Cassidy Santino. God knows, we were made for each other."

Her sighs and responses delighted him. When she answered, her own sincerity was the final delight. "I love you, too, baby. For as long as you want me, I'm yours."

"Will forever be too long?"

"Not in this lifetime."

"Good! Then we'll book in for the next go-around too. I can't imagine ever wanting another woman this way. Just won't happen."

She stared into his eyes; hers full of passion, no doubt mirroring his. The deep blue glittered with sexual delight as he strove to control his own release in order to pleasure her first. She moved with him, her breathing labored, her smile tender.

"Trace, my love, you're the most beautiful man I've ever met. You make me so happy…"

Oh, God!!

Chapter Fifty-five

The morning started with a strange buzzing sound that woke Cass from a dream where she and Trace were caring for a baby, him pushing a carriage while she walked next to him, her arm through his. Like a fantasy movie of a happy family, the scene had given her incredible pleasure.

Wide awake in seconds, Cass nudged Trace. "Honey, I think it's your cellphone." She unwound herself from his embrace and shook him.

He swung his naked legs from under the cover, sat up and reached for the small object making so much noise. "Hey, Diane, what's up?"

Still prone, her arms behind her head, Cass watched his expression veer from pleasant and questioning to pissed off and all business.

"I'm on my way. I'll call you from the car for the exact location. Was anyone killed?"

Cass shot to a sitting position. From the way he

wouldn't look at her, she sensed an involvement.

Trace hung up, grabbed for his pants and began to get dressed. "I gotta go, honey. Sorry." While he buttoned his shirt, stuffed it into his pants and threaded the belt through, she flung herself toward the closet to get her robe. "What happened, Trace?"

"They were transporting a few of the prisoners from the detention center to the jail and someone hijacked the vehicle, broke the prisoners out and killed the driver and the guard."

"Oh, no. That's horrible. How many convicts escaped?"

"Two. Both killers. The city's on high-alert." He threaded his hands through hair in need of a cut and looked as if he was trying to make up his mind how much more he could share. Finally, he came to her and swept her into his arms.

His kiss branded her and she felt herself swaying from the effect.

"Baby, I want you to stay home and keep the doors locked. Could you call in sick tonight?"

"No can do, bud. I promised Rusty I'd work with Arlene today. She has a championship bout coming soon that he's fast-tracked her for and she needs to ramp up the training. Why would you even suggest that?"

"Cassi, I'm not kidding. You need to be extra careful."

She leaned back and stared at his hooded

expression. Her stomach dropped. "What aren't you telling me?"

"One of the escapees is your good friend, Juan Acedo."

Lord... seriously?

Chapter
Fifty-six

Cass appeased Trace by agreeing to call in sick for her shift at the club. But no way would she let Rusty down. Not when he'd specifically asked for her help over the next few days. To further calm the tiger, she did promise to be on guard and not to ride her bike to the gym. She'd drive her Mustang and park it in the back lot, take all the precautions she could, yet life had to go on.

He'd listened to her justification and wavered; more after she'd reminded him that she'd be surrounded by fighters and that Rusty would die before he'd let anyone hurt her.

Leaving her with a kiss she'd remember for some time and a playful smack on the rump, along with his teasing warning of "Be careful, sugar" still ringing in her ear, she gathered herself together and organized her belongings.

Glad that the cut on her arm had closed from the

stitches, ointment and bandage Sam had used to doctor the wound; she changed the dressing for a smaller one and donned a red top with sleeves that hid it.

A little later, she pulled up behind the gym in one of the few parking spaces Rusty's had tagged and checked all around her. Spooked from Trace's earlier behavior, she made sure the back lot was empty before leaving the safety of the Mustang.

When Trace had told her about Juan's foul play with his mother, she'd put two and two together and decided that Juan must have come straight to her place after he'd done the deed. She remembered his morose attitude that night, how it had freaked her out, chilled her so she'd wanted him gone. She recalled him telling her he'd needed a friend.

Not sure how she felt about his part in the mercy killing, her first reaction had been anger, blood boiling anger. How could he have murdered a sick, defenceless woman? Then remembering Kathleen's condition, she came to see her death in a different light.

Was that how Mary had convinced her son to carry out this horrific deed? Had she done so before? According to Trace, all Mary's patients died. Ah, but then, in her defence, all her patients *had* been terminally ill. The question left unanswered was whether she'd used her son as a mercy killer for those people.

Cass shook off her gloomy thoughts and gathered her gear. *I guess I can't sit in judgement in this case. I'll leave that to a jury. Poor Juan! I'm beginning to think the guy never stood a chance.*

Rusty met her at the door, his eyebrow raised. "Why're you coming in the back door, Brat?"

"Trace made me promise to be extra careful today." Cass saw Arlene step up next to Rusty so she nodded and got the same in return. "Hi, Arlene."

"Hey! What's up? Why'd you use the back lot and not the side one where the rest of us lowlifes have to park?"

Cass didn't believe that Arlene gave a damn if she chose the rear lot but she didn't want to put her student in a bad mood before they'd even entered the ring. So she answered. "Detective Maguire warned me there were a couple of killers loose in the city. They'd escaped from a prison van earlier today and the two guards were killed in the getaway. One of the convicts we all know, Juan Acedo."

Cass noticed Rusty's attempt to balance Arlene when she reacted to Cass's announcement. She also saw the other slap at his hand and mutter, "I tripped. I'm okay. Don't paw me."

Instantly suspicious, anger flooding, she pushed against Arlene's chest. "What's up with the attitude? Rusty was only being a gentleman."

Arlene glared from one to the other and headed

for the ring, "I don't need anyone's help."

Rusty stopped Cass from taking things further. "She's been in a rotten mood all morning, brat. But the dame's worked her ass off too. Something's burrowed up her butt and of course, being Arlene, she won't share. God help me; give me strength to deal with crazy females."

"Hey!"

"Present company excluded, of course."

Cass grinned and winked. "I loosened up in the home gym, Rus. I'm raring to start whenever you are."

He looked relieved. "Okay, great! Go get ready, doll. We wouldn't want to keep her royal pain in the ass-ness waiting too long."

Cass changed into her boxing gear and for the next hour she concentrated on working Arlene hard, making her pay attention to every clue she could think of teaching her.

Once Arlene learned to sense her opponent's next ploy, the better fighter she'd be. It wasn't easy teaching her to know where and how an opponent would come at her. Being born with that instinct, that's what made the difference between a good fighter and a great one.

Finally, Rusty called a halt and had the girls cool down with stretching exercises while he nattered at Arlene about how well she'd done. Soon, though, he warned her about how her cocky ways would get her in trouble.

"Yer just not as good as you think you are, brat. But, you've come a long way."

Cass watched Arlene and saw how pleased she'd looked from Rusty's endearment. One he only used for Cassi.

"I'm feeling great, Rusty. I won those last few bouts." She turned to Cass. "You weren't there but both fights were knockouts, easy ones. Tell her, old man."

He stepped up behind Arlene who sat on the bench and faced Cass, his expression comical. "Yeah, kid. You did good... both knockouts were in the second round when I told you to play with them for at least four. Yep! You did *real* good."

Cassi couldn't help it. She laughed and loved it when Arlene ducked her head to hide her own smile.

I do believe that ole man's getting to her...

Cass was used to the guys in the gym ignoring them. Even the few females who'd become regulars paid little attention. None of the women were serious fighters and had joined the gym as an exercise facility. Up until today when a new girl had hovered the whole time they'd gone through their workout. Now she lurked as if wanting to start a conversation.

Arlene inched forward and spoke in a low voice, forcing both Cass and Rusty to lean in so they could hear her. "Hey, Rus, that nosy bitch over there, is that Ariana Wilde?"

"Yeah. She's been watching the whole time. Likely, wants to see what competition she'll have for the state championship. Can't throw her out; she paid to use the exercise equipment. Besides, I wanted to observe her moves. She lifts seventy-five pounds like it's a small bag of flour for crissakes, doesn't even look winded. And her skipping footwork is smooth, tireless, plus she knocks the hell out of the punching bag—more like a guy than a dame. That broad can hit hard. You're going to have a fight on your hands, Arlene. It won't be an easy knock-out like your last two. I'm thinking we're pushing this too fast, kid. I'm thinking to cancel."

Arlene's face hardened and her voice ground the ice chips that had formed. "Don't you dare! I can take her. You know I can."

"Sure, I know you can. The question is—do *you* know it?"

Cass interrupted the two bickerers. "She's coming over."

Ariana strode over and stopped in front of Cass. "I'm looking forward to our dance coming up, sugar."

"I'm not your dance partner. Arlene is." Cass stepped back so Arlene was included in the circle.

Ariana flicked a disdainful glance her way and turned back to Cass. "I'd rather fight you."

Feeling Arlene stiffen, knowing she'd be in the other's face within seconds, Cass answered. "I'm

Arlene's sparring partner, nothing more. She's the fighter."

"Her?" Disdain flooded Ariana's face. Her attitude shouted disrespect and Rusty had to haul on Arlene's arm to stop her from making a move.

Not wanting to overshadow her, Cass shot Ariana a mocking grin and added. "You think you're good enough?"

Ariana stiffened and a sneer appeared. She grinned back, sharing it with all three of them. "Oh yeah. Not only do I *know* I'm good enough, I'm better."

Cass threaded her arm through Arlene's and turned them toward the change rooms. After a few steps where she force-walked Arlene away from the confrontation, she stopped and turned. She only said one sentence and watched Ariana's sneering expression fade while Rusty crowed.

"I wouldn't put my money on it, Arlene's the best."

Chapter
Fifty-seven

Trace arrived at the crime scene within a short time and could see that his crew had cordoned off the area. Gawkers were gathered behind the barriers, everyone's cameras flashing. The crazy world today had instant replays and their bloody phones gave them the ability to record real-time events.

As he approached the area, he made out that one of the escort officers had been shot in the driver's seat while the other had been forced to the rear of the vehicle to release the two detainees before taking a bullet.

Peering into the car window, splattered with the blood of the poor guy just doing his slightly above minimum wage job, Trace felt anger rise up and almost choke him. The viciousness of the attack stunned the hell out of him, making him wonder who could have wanted the prisoners freed this much that two lives were worth the cost.

He glanced around the area and saw the possibility of feedback from the ATM machine at the corner and the street cams in the vicinity. Plus there were a few visible store fronts where they might get lucky.

Diane slid up to him, her notebook in her hand. "I know, get the coverage. Already on it. Not sure it'll do much good though. Man over there said he saw the whole thing play out." She pointed to a ball-capped, bearded fellow in his mid-forties who looked to be a dependable witness.

"What'd he say?" Trace headed in his direction with Diane rushing to keep up.

"Two people involved is what he saw. They drove an unlicensed SUV, black Honda CR-V. No license plate, tinted windows. They wore dark clothes, used black Balaclavas and blue rubber gloves."

"He's got nothing else?"

"Nope. He says they never spoke that he could hear."

"After they got the two out, what happened?"

"Guess they hustled them into the SUV and took off. Slick as snot. Easy does it because no one expected it to happen."

"Bastards!"

"You know what, Trace? This is getting personal. Two of ours dead. Oh yeah! It's personal."

"You figure it's the *Armas* bunch taking Juan?"

"The other guy's a loner. Tried to rob a casino to get his money back and his gun went off accidently. Or so he says."

"Therefore, no one would go to the trouble of breaking him out."

"Right."

"So that leaves Juan, the mercy killer."

"Yep. I figure that sick hairy bastard must have been their target."

Chapter
Fifty-eight

After Ariana disappeared, Cass left Rusty and Arlene planning their strategy for the next fight. She'd gotten used to arranging to be in the showers either before or after Arlene and today was no different.

Since they'd always clashed, it seemed less conflicting and somehow smarter to stay out of the other girl's way. It often bothered her that Arlene held such animosity towards her. She wished she knew why.

Right from the beginning, on the first day they met and scrapped over Cass's aversion to Arlene's bitchiness to Rusty, they'd had trouble finding even ground. No matter how hard she had to work at keeping the peace, she'd do it for her old friend.

But as far as Arlene was concerned, she owed the other girl nothing. According to Rusty, it was the other way around. Arlene should thank her lucky stars for having Cass to train with her. The only reason she put herself in the ring with Arlene most days was for Rusty's sake. He'd asked for a favor and she'd never refuse that old man anything that was in her power to give. So she'd put up with Arlene's snarky ways.

Although, she'd sensed a slight change in the other girl's attitude today and not wanting to push her luck, she'd backed off. Instead, she shut off her shower when Arlene appeared with her towel and made her way back to where her clothes hung waiting.

Once dressed, she headed out to find Rusty. "Same time tomorrow?"

"Yeah, good." He gestured with his thumb toward the room she'd just came from. "She's settling into her stride, Cass. Man, she can fight. I knew she had potential and you've worked wonders with her."

"Glad to help, my friend. You know, every once in a while she makes me remember sparring with Raoul. He could be predictable yet I could never take him for granted. He'd change up and catch me out until I'd learned to stop second guessing him and let my instincts take over."

Rusty laughed. "I guess that's one of the talents all good boxers possess. The ability to reel in their opponent and then level 'em. Ha! Your dad had that in spades. Won a lot of his fights that way."

"I'm glad I never had the urge to be a fighter,

Rus. I love the sport; don't get me wrong, but never as a career."

"And yet, kiddo, you could be one of the greats. No doubt about it. You work harder at keeping your body in shape than many of the serious fighters."

Cassi grinned. "Because I'm a superficial chick who likes to look good."

"Bullshit! You don't have a conceited bone in your body. Quit trying to fake a faker, brat. Off with you now. See you tomorrow."

Cass squeezed him with a side-arm hug and retreated before his shyness kicked in. Planning a trip to the hospital next, she decided to step across the street to the florist shop so she could pick up a nice bouquet of flowers for Faith.

Not paying attention to anyone nearby, she didn't see the man who stepped off the curb behind her, nor did she expect to feel the muzzle of a gun in her back.

Chapter
Fifty-nine

Arlene stepped out of the gym, feeling on top of the world. Everything had a rhythm in the ring and she'd found hers today. Her moves flowed together like a well-choreographed dance. Warming up with the speedball, her punches had a tempo to them that had taken her a long time to perfect.

Then in the ring with Cass, she'd executed her footwork as if she had a musical beat playing in her head. Swaying, dipping, her well-oiled body moving like the machine she'd worked so hard to develop, she'd felt the love for the sport overtake her until that high of doing exactly what she was born to do kicked in.

For the first time in a very long while, she felt on top of the world. Later, that would be her one excuse for turning away when she'd seen Juan Acedo move in behind Cass, a gun in his hand and trouble on his mind.

He hadn't shot her outright, which told her the man had plans. Sure as hell, he was forcing Cass to walk toward a white minivan he'd parked across the street.

Arlene hurried to her bike, Mani's precious gift, and donned her helmet. Then she wheeled that motorcycle around and peeled out of the parking lot toward the street, the roar of its power making her heart sing in the same way it always did.

She hit the street with a skid, wheeled to the right and drove between the two people in front of her, forcing Juan to jump out of the way or get run over. If she could have, she'd have grabbed the gun out of his hands but he'd dropped it, panicky to save his life.

Slowing, she screamed at Cass. "Get on, girl. We've got to leave."

Not needing a second invitation, Cass hopped on behind her, wrapped her arms around Arlene's stomach and kicked at Juan who'd made a last minute lunge to stop her from getting away.

The two flew to the corner, both leaning into the turn and Arlene heard Cass's hysteria in her laugh as they spun out before she righted the huge machine.

Arlene checked her mirror and saw Juan's van following behind them and knew she'd have to do some pretty fancy maneuvering around the city to lose the jerk. Good thing she knew of some streets where a bike would be able to take trails that a car couldn't follow.

She heard Cass's voice and knew the girl wasn't talking to her. She had her phone. Good, she's thinking. Hopefully, she'll get the cops in on the chase before too long.

The van's sudden appearance on her left had her shift into a higher gear, dangerously taking a right turn at the last minute. As the bike flew around the corner, Arlene's body stiffened. Cass's legs tightened around her thighs, revealing the other had ridden passenger before.

They lost the van for a block. By the time they hit the next corner, he re-appeared.

Cass yelled into her ear, "I called 911, said there was a crazy following us. They told me to head to the police station off the highway and they'd intercept."

"Okay. Hang on."

Arlene hit the next corner, ran the red light and headed for one of the streets where she knew lay a switchback. It came up fast and she had no time to warn Cass. With a leap over a curb, she aimed the bike along a narrow trail that headed downhill, flooding out onto the street below. Praying no cars would be there when they cleared the buildings; she breathed a sigh of relief when the road appeared empty.

They flew out onto the street just in time to cut off a souped-up Hummer who she knew belonged to none other than Sergio Mandalas. From her days with the *Armas* gang, Arlene had gotten to know a lot about their competition.

Flying along the highway, feeling foolishly secure because they'd lost Juan; she slowed down until Cass tightened her hold. "There he is. He's coming up alongside of us."

Sure as shit, Juan had cut across the desert-like field and was gaining fast. Once again, Arlene gunned it only to have him pull up on the right shoulder, his gun aimed at Cass. He screamed, "Stop now or I shoot Cass. I mean it. Pull over."

Shit! He'd do it too. Arlene slowed, pulled over and shut off the motor.

Cass whispered. "I'll step off and you ride for help. He won't shoot me. Go."

"Yeah, like that's gonna happen. He might not shoot you, but he'll put a bullet in my back faster than you could say don't."

"I'll stop him. Go."

"Too late!"

Arlene left her helmet on and prayed the son of a bitch didn't recognize her. If he did, she'd lay money he'd extract his vengeance for her leaving him. And she'd win.

As he jammed on his brakes, Juan's tires spit up dirt from the roadside. With his gun in sight, held out front, he hurried toward the girls.

Arlene stepped away from Cass, hoping she'd get a chance to attack if his attention centered on the other girl for long enough.

"Why did you run away?" He held the gun on Arlene while he questioned Cass. She looked relaxed and unafraid. Arlene had to admit to a feeling of admiration for her gym partner. "You said we were friends."

"Are you kidding me? That was before you killed Katherine McGuire. Besides, friends don't come after each other with guns."

"I never killed her. My mother did. You let me down."

"And you're scaring the shit outta me so I guess we're even. Look, Juan. Let Arlene go. This is between us."

"Arlene?" His head swiveled her way and his voice changed, no longer coaxing or caring. Hatred had its own nuance and his tone rang with it. He turned to her. "Take off your helmet, bitch."

Heart sinking, praying she wouldn't disgrace herself by begging; she removed the helmet and shook out her hair. Then she stared at him, making sure no sign of the fear rampaging inside could be seen in the sneer on her face. "Hi, Baby."

Chapter Sixty

Trace heard the car radio burst to life as one of the police officers he knew well called in a report. "Trace there's a 911 call from Cassidy Santino. She mentioned your name, said she was being followed, identified Juan Acedo. We dispatched some officers and figured you might like to be in on this one." He gave directions of where they'd last seen the chase and disconnected.

Diane looked his way from the passenger side of their SUV, her expression tight. "We're close, Trace. We'll find them. Tracking the scanner, they listened in real time as the cops revealed their destination.

Trace did a u-turn that earned him a blast of acid in his gut and a grunted cuss word from Diane. When they arrived at the place where Cass had left her last transmission, other cop cars were pulled over next to an empty white van. The men circled something lying in the ditch.

The staccato hammering of his heart and his weak knees made getting out of his car one of the hardest things Trace ever had to do. Not sure of what he'd find, scared beyond anything he'd ever felt before in his life, he raced towards the group of officers.

On the ground a woman's motorcycle helmet lay near a small pool of blood.

Nothing else.

Chapter Sixty-one

Cass stiffened. *Baby? They knew each other. Of course they did. Arlene had been in the gang.*

"I thought you'd left town a long time ago. I searched everywhere."

"Yeah, well. Shit happens."

"Mani got you out. He made a deal with Dani. I heard the rumors. Why'd you leave?" Juan kept the gun on Arlene. Smart, he shielded it with his body in case any traffic went by. He must have sensed that Cassi wouldn't make a move if he threatened the other girl.

"I gotta spell it out for you?"

"I thought you liked me? That we were a couple."

"Nah! You never let me breathe, Juan. It was time to make a life on my own. I tried to tell you I hated being in the gang. You didn't pay attention. You gave me no choice. I had to run."

While Cassi listened to the ongoing

conversation, she noticed that Sergio Mandala's Hummer had driven past on the other side of the split highway. She'd also seen a signal from the passenger window. A hand appeared signalling five. She sincerely hoped he meant minutes. Then she saw the Hummer in the distance disappear onto a side road.

Arlene's voice brought Cass's attention back to the scene unfolding in front of her. The other girl had run away from Juan. Cass could understand that concept. The stalker never let up.

Juan pulled a couple of plastic ties from his pocket and handed one to Arlene.

"Put your hands behind you, Cass. Then Arlene will tie this around them. Do it now."

Cass turned and scanned the area. "It's okay, Arlene. Do as he says."

Arlene stepped behind her and secured it in place.

"Pull it tight, bitch."

"Shut up, Juan, or do it yourself."

Cass made a cautionary sound toward Arlene. Then she added, "Do as he says, Arlene. It's fine."

"Arlene. Get over here and turn around."

Arlene took her time going toward Juan. Once she was a couple of feet away, she pulled one of her ringside dance routines where she skipped her feet, swayed her body and dropped her shoulders doing the dip and jerk movement. Stunned, Juan backed away and let his gun hand drop. That's all

Arlene needed. Her fist shot out and caught him in the solar plexus. Another caught him in his face. A spurt of blood flew from his nose as he dropped to the ground.

"Quick, Cass. Let's go." Arlene retrieved the gun and after checking it over, in what looked like a fit of temper, she chucked it across the field at least thirty feet. Not waiting for a second invitation, Cass headed in her direction. She stopped when the Hummer pulled up alongside her and Sergio got out.

Taking in the scene at a glance, he could see Juan struggle to pick his head up from the gravel and he also saw Arlene start her bike, then turn to wait.

"Go Cassi. I've got this."

Cass hesitated for a few seconds. Long enough for Sergio to pull his knife and cut off the bindings around her wrists. Two of the guys in his vehicle lifted Juan and began dragging him away.

"Go on now."

A knowing came over Cass and she started to argue. Then she heard Juan scream her name. "No can do, Sergio. Let him go."

"Are you kidding me, man? He was going to kidnap you. Hell, do you honestly believe he would have released you after the kinds of things he planned to do to you? Grab a brain, girl."

Arlene pulled the bike up beside Cass, her motor roaring and her frustration obvious.

"It's not our business, Cass. Leave it alone. Let's

get the hell out of here while they'll still let us." She glanced at Sergio and the fearful respect she had for the other gang leader was evident.

Juan's screams now muffled, Cass stepped closer to Sergio. "Promise me you'll deliver him to the LVPD."

"You got it. Now get the fuck outta here before they show up on the scene. Can't you hear the sirens? Go!"

Arlene revved the motor for incentive and Cass leapt on the back of the bike. Whirling the macho machine like a pro, Arlene drove across the field to connect to the highway going the opposite way, heading back to town. Noisy cop cars and a black SUV with lights flashing sped past.

Chapter
Sixty-two

Arlene parked in front of Cassi's house and shut off the engine. The two sat together for a few seconds without saying a word. Then Cass lifted her arms from around Arlene's waist to tighten around her shoulders. She gave her a swift hug. "Thank you for coming back and helping me."

Stiff now, pulling away, Arlene got off the bike as if she needed to put distance between them. "Yeah, well, you'd have done the same for me. Besides, if Rusty ever found out I left his brat with a madman, he'd drop me this fast." To make her point, she snapped her finger and thumb together, the loud sound making a point.

"And that would be the end of the world?" Cass had to know.

"For me, yes. I need this sport in my life. It gives it meaning. I was lost until I stumbled into the gym." Realizing she had shared more than she wanted, her lips closed tight and a grimace flashed over her features.

Not wanting to upset her further, Cass changed the subject. "Come inside for some dinner. I'll make you the best lasagna you've ever tasted."

Before Arlene's shocked pleasure could fade, a taxi pulled up in front of them and a man got out. One glance and delight engulfed Cass. "Billy!"

He turned at the sound of his name and held out his arms, his new physique a total reversal of the broken man she'd last seen. His streaked auburn hair looked thick, shiny and clean, well-groomed the way he'd always wore it in the early days when he'd been compulsive in his expensive styles. The weight he'd gained now gave his medium-height a healthy and muscular appearance rather than gaunt and sickly like he'd been before his treatment.

She ran to give him his requested hug and he spun her off her feet, rationalizing happiness as the reason for the tremors she felt passing through his body.

"They let you come home."

"It's been a couple of months, Cassi. I'm clean and ready to start living again. Plus, I couldn't stop thinking about you. That you needed me strong and healthy to help you find Raoul's killers."

Stomach dropping, not wanting to have this conversation, she clutched his hand and turned him in Arlene's direction before the other could leave as she was obviously planning to do. "Wait, Arlene. I'd like you to meet a friend of mine."

Stunned, her normal clear-eyed gaze shifty, Arlene spoke before Cass could introduce them. "Hi, Mr. Duran."

"Hello, Arlene. How's life?"

"Changed." Arlene glanced toward Cass, her expression cold and indifferent—back to normal. She muttered, "See you around." In seconds, she disappeared, leaving Cass dumbfounded.

"Sorry, Billy. That girl's got the biggest chip on her shoulder of anyone I've ever met."

"Didn't look like that to me when we pulled up and you were hugging her." His voice registered a note that made Cass uncomfortable yet not sure why it would. Not being able to put her finger on whether it was condemnation or jealousy, she decided she was imagining things and let it go. After all, there'd never been any kind of a relationship between her and Billy except that of big brother and naïve, shy adopted sister.

"She knew you, didn't she?"

"What do you mean?" He stared at her, his gray eyes guarded.

"She called you by your name, Mr. Duran."

"I met a lot of people in and around the courts, Cassi. In those days, people showed respect."

Not sure why this explanation didn't ring true, Cass let it go. After all, it made sense that Arlene could have known Billy during his career as a lawyer. She just didn't believe it was the explanation for the absolute panic oozing from her sparring partner.

"Look, come in and I'll make you dinner. Just give me a minute to grab a quick shower, check in with work and call a friend."

"Do you have lasagna and chocolate cake?"

Laughing, Cassi nodded. "Lasagna, yes. Cake no. I do have some Oreo cookies. They'll have to satisfy you."

Billy waved off the cab driver, lifted a small backpack and wrapped his arm around Cass's shoulders to guide her to the house. "Honey, now that I'm out of that prison and back with you, I'm a hundred percent happy. I'm thinking the satisfaction will follow soon."

Chapter Sixty-three

Trace and Diane were still at the scene when his phone rang. As soon as he heard the dial tone, heart beating double-time, astonished joy in his voice, he answered, "Cassi, baby. You got away from him."

"I'm fine, Trace. Arlene came along just in time on Mani's motorcycle and she helped me escape."

"How do you know it was Mani's bike?"

"He had his name air-brushed over the fender. Why do you ask?"

"Hell if I know. It just came out. Did the son of a bitch hurt you?"

Scrambling, not wanting to admit the truth about their close call, Cassi hedged. "No. He's dead."

"Juan's dead?"

"No, Mani. So he couldn't hurt us. I'm getting mixed up, aren't I?"

"Cass, I'm on the side of the highway where we found a pool of blood and a woman's motorcycle helmet. Across the field, one of the officers also found a gun. You've got to talk to me. We'll need you to make a statement."

"Sure, okay. Can we do it later? I have a friend visiting for a little while and we're going to sit down to dinner. Sam says I don't have to come in because Juan's still missing so I'll be waiting for you."

"Okay. We'll clean up here and I'll be over. If Juan is still out there somewhere, I want to set up protection for you. An unmarked vehicle will be parked outside your house in a few minutes. And I'll be there as soon as I can."

"Don't panic, Trace. Billy Duran is with me now. We're catching up on old times. So there's no need to worry."

"Yeah? Well. Damned if I know why that news isn't making me feel a whole lot better?"

Chapter Sixty-four

Arlene rode around for some time before pulling the bike into her aunt's driveway. A niggling voice had been narking at her since the funeral. It was past time to check on her poor, sick uncle.

Leaving the bike on the side, she made her way to the front door and rang the bell. Her I-don't-give-a-shit attitude shifted into place for protection as she waited for her aunt's sarcasm once she opened the door.

"Arlene. You came back." Her surprise showed pleasure rather than disgust and it stunned Arlene speechless. All she could do was nod.

"Your uncle will be pleased. He was asking after you and I had no way of getting in touch. He's better since he saw you last."

Arlene stepped across the threshold and knew her aunt was relatively sober, not like the day of Mani's funeral.

"Would you like a glass of wine? Or you could join us for dinner? It's not much, just meatloaf but you used to like it?"

Not knowing what had happened to make her aunt change from the bitch she'd portrayed after the funeral to the welcoming hostess today left Arlene feeling like the ground under her feet wasn't solid. Seeing no other choice, she played along. "Sure. I haven't eaten. Thanks."

"That's good. If you go up and sit with Phil, I'll bring a tray upstairs for all of us and we'll eat together. It'll be like old times."

Arlene went to her uncle's bedroom, knocked and peeked around the open door. "Anyone up for a visitor?"

"Leni. Sweetheart, you kept your promise and came back." He held out his hands for her to come near and give him a hug. "I told Barbara you would. She'll be so happy to see you too."

"Not so sure about that, Uncle Phil, but I knew you'd be pleased." After they hugged, Arlene sat on the side of his bed where he patted. "You're lolling today, she teased. Aren't you feeling very well?"

"It's one of my bad days. Or it was until I saw your pretty face. Is Barbara coming to join us?"

"She's getting dinner ready and says we'll eat in here with you."

"Good! She's been under a huge amount of pressure lately. As you know, she built an incredible business and because I'm not well, she's been running it from the house. Since we lost Mani, we've spent a lot of time together and we've talked more in these last weeks than we have for years. I'm not too ashamed to admit, we did a fair amount of crying too. Over lost opportunities, mostly. Barbara broke down and admitted to her jealously having to share Mani and me with you and she's sickened by the way she's treated you in the past. We want you to be a part of our lives again, Leni. You mustn't stay away for such long stretches. We need to know that you're okay. And you need to know that you're our little girl and will always be a part of this family."

Exhausted from his lecture and the emotion it took for him to explain and defend his wife's behavior, tears rolled down his cheeks. His trembling hands hadn't stopped fluttering around to emphasize his honesty and the importance of his words. His white hair had slid over onto his forehead, leaving a curl hanging in the rakish way it used to when he was a much younger man.

It touched her heart and she softened. The hard core built over the last few years shifted and remorse began to simmer.

"I'll come and see you as much as I can, you old softie you. I promise."

His eyes lit, the bluish white in his pupils darkened with happiness. "I'll hold you to that, Leni. It'll be a treat for me to look forward to."

In a very short while, her aunt carried in a tray with three filled plates, a pitcher of water with glasses and cutlery. She passed everyone their dinner and pulled up the chair on the other side of the bed. "Now isn't this nice?"

Not sure what to think, Arlene smiled and nodded. Then she ate everything on her plate. At first, the talk flowed between her Aunt and Uncle. Soon they asked her questions, and with some coaxing, she admitted to having a new direction.

Neither of them seemed too taken with her being a boxer, it was clear in their reactions. But her Uncle insisted that they supported her right to choose. Her aunt hid her expression by rolling her lips together to force them shut. Arlene, engrossed in her tale, shared more than she'd intended and soon, her aunt began to nod as she listened to how one built a career in the ring.

Talking about the upcoming battles she'd be forced to win so she'd have a chance at a championship bout, Arlene relaxed in a way she hadn't for a long time.

Delighted with the sense of family, Arlene knew it was the first time since she'd left this house that she felt safe. Except, one huge problem hung over her like a full-fledged tornado funnel.

Juan was on the loose again and he knew she was in town. That she had come from Rusty's gym with her bike. And she was an acquaintance of Cassidy Santino's.

What she didn't know was what Sergio Mandala's boys were going to do with him? Shock followed shock today. First she'd put herself in danger to save Cass, and if the truth be known, she hadn't hesitated.

Then she'd had a face to face with Juan, the creep she'd been running from since the old days.

And even more strange, Sergio Mandalas the menacing boss of the *Los Soldados* knew Cass. He'd told her to leave Juan with them and she'd *argued*. With the one man in Vegas – that every gang member no matter which posse one belonged to – would rather cut a vein than oppose.

Mandalas was one mean mother and no one had the balls to stand up to him. Well, except for Cass. And, the bastard had listened to her. He'd gotten his way, but he'd still listened. Only problem, Arlene had already started the Harley and hadn't heard what he'd said.

Thinking harder, Arlene wondered if Sergio would let Juan go. If he knew the truth of what went down the night Raoul was shot, maybe not. The thing was – Juan would never tell them the truth. He'd willingly give her up as the shooter to save his own sorry ass. And he had the fingerprints on her gun, the one that had shot Raoul, to prove his story.

If Sergio believed Juan was innocent, would he let Juan walk? She'd been out of the loop for a long time. Buried her head in the sands of who-gives-a-shit and had no real idea of what had been happening in that sick world since she left. A revolting queasiness began, churning the food she'd just eaten. Questions popped up that recalled that same ugly fear she thought she'd left behind.

Would Juan have Mani's address?

Would he come looking for her here?

Would God be that cruel?

Chapter
Sixty-five

"While I was away, I dreamed of your lasagna, Cassi and it was every bit as good as I remembered." Sitting next to each other on the sofa, Billy reached for her hand and his thumb smoothed the skin on top.

"Good. Next time you're here, I'll have a chocolate cake in the freezer for you too. Not that you had trouble wolfing down those four cookies one after the other. Not that I was counting."

"Four, huh? And you weren't counting? Truth is I ate five. I snarfed another one when you were filling the dishwasher."

Laughing, happy to see Billy behaving like his old self, she started to discuss the elephant in the room they'd pushed into the corner. "So, Billy, tell me the truth. Do you feel ready to tackle life again? Have you come to terms with the trial?"

"Which one are you referring to, Cassi?"

What? "The one that made you lose faith in the system."

"Faith? Oh, right. The Blackwell case. Yeah, I've laid those ghosts to rest."

Cassi tugged on her hand and then used both to rub her thighs. She noticed his confusion over her question and it shocked her. Had he forgotten what had started his downhill slide into the world of drugs? In those days, he'd been a high-powered lawyer and had begun to make a name for himself. Then this notorious case had come along where his genius defence had gotten a killer off. Three days later they arrested Blackwell again. This time he'd raped and killed a little girl called Susie Roland.

When it happened, Billy'd come to their place a lot, heart-sore about his part in freeing the devil. They'd listened and tried to soothe his pain. After all, he'd grown up in the neighborhood, worked three jobs to get through college and lived with them a lot over the last year in school while studying to pass the bar exam. When Cassi's dad won the big fight, he'd paid Billy's final semester of tuition after Billy's own mother stole his college funds and used it for drugs.

They were family and Billy had brother status. Once he'd begun working for a prestigious law firm, they hadn't seen nearly as much of him. By then, his hours were deadly and being happy for him, they accepted that he'd moved on.

After the Roland debacle, he'd decided he

needed a change, get the Vegas desert out of his pores and start over in L.A. During those next years, they were lucky to get a phone call over Christmas and that was often a few days late. According to Newsweek and other magazines, Billy lived a lavish lifestyle and had found success.

Until, he lost it.

According to the sad story he shared after his return, he'd tried to let go of the guilt, of knowing he'd let a monster free. But it ate away at him until he couldn't sleep or eat, or even think. He'd gotten into drugs and his downfall became inevitable.

She'd lost touch after the first few times he stolen money from them. Raoul had kicked him out, ordering him to find a place of his own and no more mooching.

Now here he was. And he looked good. "I'm so thankful you made this choice, Billy, to get your life back."

"I know, hey? I guess it's true about the flames of hell burning a fool before he sees the light. And that one has to have a reason to overcome one's failings. For me, it was you being alone after Raoul died. I knew you'd need me."

No! Not gonna happen. Never again! "Billy, please don't take this the wrong way. I'm honored and happier than you'll ever know to see you looking so well. Realizing that you cared enough about my circumstances to fight for your life is the sweetest thing anyone has ever done for me. I love you for it."

"I sense a rebuttal coming." He wore a quirky grin yet his eyes were narrowed.

She searched for the earlier lightness that had made his gentle gray eyes sparkle. At this moment, they were soaked in the black highlights that she remembered. Ones that appeared whenever he'd been focused and determined and... ruthless. "Yes. I'm my own person now, Billy, no more little sister. I make my own choices."

Switching topics, a trick he'd always used when he didn't like the conversation, he asked, "Have they caught Raoul's killer?"

"Well, no. Not yet. They're close. I have a feeling by tonight, they'll have the case solved and we can all move on."

"How so?"

"We know there were three men at the scene. Two have since died and the third should be in custody pretty soon."

"Do you know which one was the shooter?"

"No."

"What about your stalker problem, Acedo? Has that stopped?"

"Yes. In fact, he's the one they're about to arrest again for the murder of a police detective's mother. They believe he's also Raoul's killer."

"And you're not so sure?"

"What makes you say that?"

"I know you, Cassi. And I've never known you

to lie. But right now, those blue beauties aren't being honest. It's in the way you've turned your head to hide behind your hair. By the way, have I told you how very attractive you look?"

Feeling uncomfortable with his personal remarks and not wanting to discuss the case so callously, she closed down. "Thanks. So, what's your plans now, Billy?"

Taking her hint serious, he dropped the subject of the murder and answered her question instead. "I contacted a friend who's running his own small law firm here in town. He's looking for a good lawyer who'll work cheap. Since, I've got no choice; I'll be his mule and put in the hours for as long as it takes to get my foot back in the door. My problem is, I don't have any money to get outfitted for the position. And I have no place to live—"

Not sure if Billy was hinting at staying with her, she set him straight when she cut him off. "That's no problem. I have a few hundred in cash for a motel for now and I'll write you a check to cover the cost of new clothes and an apartment. No, don't argue."

He'd held his hand up and she cut off whatever he'd been about to say.

"Let me do this for you, my friend. It will be worth every penny if you can get your old life back."

Not understanding the hard note that entered his voice when he answered, or the shiver that attacked her from his tone, nonetheless, she was happy with his words.

"Oh, honey, you can bet on it that'll I'll get my old life back. I'll pay you and everyone else what I owe, I promise. No matter what it takes."

Chapter
Sixty-six

Billy didn't want to leave when Cass began hinting for him to go. In fact, if he hadn't seen it for himself, he'd have never believed that Cassidy Santino could have changed so drastically from the easily manipulated, soft-hearted girl he'd once known to the chick who'd faced him tonight.

This woman was no-one's fool. He'd have to rethink his game and play his cards differently than he'd intended. Lay low until he'd gotten his revenge on those who'd been the real reason for his past misery. Then he'd make his move.

Being the one female he'd always wanted and couldn't have; Cassi'd never left his thoughts. Back in the days when he'd been on top, women were a dime a dozen, most he couldn't even recall.

But they'd never satisfied his thirst. The only one who could do that was the girl who'd just given him a check for five thousand dollars. She hadn't hesitated, as if she was daring him. Here's your choice, man. Live the good life or hit the streets with one hell of a "goodbye Billy" party.

He remembered the angel from the old days and how hard it had been to keep his hands to himself. Her body had always been hot, even inside the dumpy clothes she'd chosen to wear back then. Nothing could hide that sweet ass, or the breasts that filled every blouse. Or her skin that he knew was as soft as the velvet of a rose petal to the touch.

It had been fear that had played a huge part in him curbing his instincts to take what he wanted. Fear of her two bruiser protectors, plus the necessity to stay in their good graces. After all, he'd known Raoul for years, they grew up together. And his unsophisticated pal had been so proud of his lawyer buddy.

When Raoul had money, he'd pay for most of their partying and brag about Billy to all of his worthless friends. It was sweet, seeing the respect and envy of those losers. It fed his ego, big time.

And, José. Without that idiot, he would never have finished his degree. Catching the old man in bed with his drunken slut of a mother had been a bonus. He'd used Jose's guilt to get him to pay for his last year of college.

After all, it had been easy to blame the bitch for taking his savings when in fact; he'd partied on smack and gone crazy. After a couple of nights at a club, he woke up to the sick realization that he'd gambled most of the funds and the rest had gone up his nose and other places on his body along with a redhead he still couldn't remember clearly.

During those days, everyone had thought him the good boy, working three jobs for university. Fact was, he'd been selling drugs for most of the money he'd earned.

The many nights he'd been studying in the Santino living room had been a bit of a ruse. Having an incredible brain, no doubt from the old man he couldn't remember, the learning came easy. Spending those nights in Cassi's house— well it had kept him sane until he'd gotten his degree.

Then life had changed.

He gave up on the chance of ever having the woman he craved and got on with his life... the good life. Drugs, booze, women and case after case that he won easily.

And then like a bone-eating cancer, he got too greedy. He put his faith in a female fiend and disgrace and failure followed.

There was only one person to blame, Dani Andino.

Chapter
Sixty-seven

Cassi couldn't believe the relief she felt once Billy left. She'd forgotten how his energy had always sapped hers. The early years when he'd been sweet to her and thankful for her family's benevolence had been the memories she'd clung to. Of course, in those days she'd worn rose-colored glasses and her world had been small and safe.

Now faced with the man again, it all came back how much he'd changed toward the end. Those last days he'd spent with them had appeared as if he'd been in hiding. Especially after his return from L.A., he'd been impossible.

Looking at herself in the mirror while redoing her make-up, she thought about the changes in her character that had taken place over such a short time. She'd become stronger in both her body and her mind. Guess the potential had always been there, she'd just needed it activated. And the death of Raoul had been the incentive.

It's amazing how gullible she'd been about the people around her just a few months ago. Her father, a devious bastard whose self-interest never failed to come first, showed himself when she was much younger. His weapon, her protectiveness for Raoul, never failed to work in getting him whatever he wanted.

The rest of her ideals about everything from the people she knew to the life she led had been naïve to say the least and downright ignorant if the truth be known.

For instance in Billy's case, she'd latched onto the good times. She'd forgotten how short tempered and secretive he'd been at the end. Hiding his drugs and stealing money to buy more, he'd pushed the limits constantly. Until Raoul caught him in her room, robbing her old piggy bank, that had been the final straw. He'd forced him out of the house and soon Billy had ended up living on the Vegas streets.

The pain of losing Raoul had blinded her to those recollections. Overcome with grief and missing her twin, she'd clung to the boyhood friend she'd adored who'd reached out for her help. And because of those sweet memories, she hadn't hesitated.

Yet the man he'd become, the person here now wasn't young Billy. Sneaky suspicions were eating away at her devotion and they made her very uncomfortable. Billy had secrets. And something told her if she ever found out about them, she wouldn't like it one little bit.

Shaking off her brooding, she rushed around, tidying up the place. She expected Trace any minute and the anticipation made her tingle in every spot on her hungry body she hoped his lips would soon be visiting.

She heard the phone and snatched it before the second ring. "Cassi here."

"Hey, Cassi. It's Sergio. I want you to know I kept my promise and delivered Juan to the police."

"Thank you—"

"Don't thank me yet. Before we dropped him off, I questioned him about the night that Raoul was killed and he swore it wasn't him who pulled the trigger. Swore it on the life of his mom. In the end, I had to believe the sucker."

"Did he tell you who did shoot Raoul?"

"He blubbered on about some chick. Kinda verifies the other leaks we'd gotten about a bitch being there."

With her throat in her mouth, Cassi asked the question that would give her the vital closure she craved. "Tell me he gave you her name. He did, didn't he?"

"Sorry, Cass. The wacko made no sense at all. He acted like a crazy person. First, he says he killed his mom. Then he babbled on about his mother making him kill people all his life. And he'd be in the deepest pits of hell while she'd end up with the angels in heaven for saving all those poor souls from going through torture. I'm telling you, girl. I think he snapped."

Her ear caught the sounds of a key opening the front door. *Trace!* Heart beating fast, joy making her voice huskier than usual, she answered. "Actually, he wasn't messin with you Sergio. You'll be hearing all about it on the news. Look, I gotta go. Talk soon."

She heard him call her name but had to hang up before Trace would see she'd gotten a call and ask her who she'd been talking with. She couldn't tell him the truth. And she was so tired of lying that one more felt like it would be one too many.

Besides, she was heartsick at knowing Juan hadn't cleared up the mystery. No doubt, Trace would come up with an inducement in his sentence for him to give up the final name. If he was in as bad a shape as Sergio seemed to believe, that could be some time down the road.

Before she could turn around, she felt strong arms encircle her waist. The intoxicating scent she associated with Trace delighted her senses while his lips made free with her neck.

She leaned against him, letting him take her weight. Covering his wandering hands with her own, she guided them to her swollen breasts.

"Trace. It's late, I worried you wouldn't come."

"Yeah, I know. I worked my ass off to get here as

soon as I could. God, it's good to hold you, baby. After what you put me through today, I needed to see for myself that you weren't hurt."

"I'm sorry, babe. I had no idea Juan had escaped or that he would come after me. You know Arlene saved me, right?"

"Hell, woman, I don't know anything other than you're okay. Have you any idea what it's like to think of you in that maniac's clutches? Knowing the crazy man with a gun had the hots for you. Dammit all, Cassi, if he'd have been in front of me, I'd have shot him. Burning in hell couldn't be worse than what I went through today, imagining him doing whatever he wanted and you unable to stop him." While he talked, his arms tightened. Taking a deep breath became impossible. She had to wriggle and squirm so he'd loosen his grip.

Her voice soothing, she spoke the words she thought might calm his rage. "He never did get me alone, Trace. I was leaving the gym, headed across the street when he came at me with his weapon and tried to get me into his van. Just then, Arlene rode her bike up to us and she forced him to step away. I jumped on the back and we drove off."

"Yeah and he followed. We have video of him pursuing you. Then we lost sight of the chase after you hit the highway."

"He caught up to us there, forced us off the bike." In this part of the story, the truth would take a little trimming.

"And? What happened?" Trace made her face him now. He searched her expression and when she tried flipping her hair, he tucked it behind her ear. "No don't hide. Tell me."

First she grimaced and bit her lip. "Promise you won't start raving."

"Do I seem that way now?"

Cassi studied his face. A bit pale, tired and disgruntled, he appeared to have found his calm. Even his eyes weren't the dark gray of impending storms like they had been just seconds earlier.

Cass swallowed and jumped in the deep end. "Everything happened so fast, Trace. We pulled over on the edge. He'd raced up on our right side and had the weapon pointed at us so we had no choice. We stopped."

At this point, Trace's expression took on a ferocious scowl and Cassi decided to veer away from that part of the story. She didn't want him to see the horror she'd felt having the barrel pointed toward her, knowing one squeeze of Juan's finger could mean the end of her life.

"Tell me." The roughness in his voice let her know his calm had faded.

"Well, when he approached, he forced Arlene to take off her helmet and that's the shocker. Although I don't know why his recognizing her should be so strange, it shook me. After I saw her tattoo, I told you she must have been in the gang at one time, remember. I guess he knew her back then."

"It's what she confirmed a little while ago when we picked her up for questioning."

"You put Arlene in jail?" Cass began to struggle.

"No. Calm down. We found her as she was leaving her Uncle's house and Diane and I took her for a coffee. She had very little to say except to admit that they'd known each other when she'd been in the gang back in L.A. In fact, he'd become a real pest and she'd gotten sick of his harassment. By the time they'd moved to Vegas, she'd gotten so she hated being a gang member and tried to get out. Mani, her cousin made that happen. He'd become important as second in command, and as a favor to him, Dani'd released her."

"You said Arlene lived in L.A.?"

"Guess she'd ended up there after she ran away from home and no one knew where she was hiding. Once she left the gang, she shut down all ties, other than seeing Mani periodically."

"They must have been close, like me and Raoul."

"Sounds like it. She said he never talked about business so she had no idea of what had been happening in the underworld. She works as an office cleaner at night, trains during the days and fights. That's her life now."

"There's one thing that bothers me. She admitted to knowing Juan. Funny thing, he came to the gym once to meet me and he didn't recognize her."

"That doesn't surprise me. When you girls are wearing your helmets, it's hard for anyone to see your faces. What if he didn't know it was her? I think she only admitted to them being acquainted because she figured you'd tell me."

"I suppose. Did she explain what happened next?"

"Her version. Now I want to hear yours."

"There's not much left to say. He made her put a tie around my wrists first. Then he told her to stand in front of him so he could do the same to her. That's where he made his mistake. When she was close enough, she punched him and he dropped."

"And...?"

"Then she threw away his gun so we could escape."

"And, then ...? Come on, Cassi. What happened next?"

Having no idea of how much Arlene had shared, Cass had no intentions of admitting Sergio Mandala's involvement unless he already knew.

She hedged. "I don't know what you mean?"

His sigh made it evident that his temper had begun to simmer and his patience had evaporated. "*Cass!*"

Shit! He never called her by that name. Her mind spun back to earlier and the scene he would have found. The empty van, the bike helmet on the ground, the blood, the tie Sergio had cut from her wrist and no Juan. *Oh! Right! No Juan.*

"Let's see if I can facilitate your memory somewhat. According to Arlene, a friend from the old days came along and took Juan away."

"Did she recognize this friend?"

"Seemed to think you might know who it was. She couldn't' recall his name."

"I'm having the same trouble myself. By then we were ready to leave, Trace, and all we wanted to do was get out of there." She cleared her throat and added, "Can we let this go. Juan has no power over us anymore."

"Right! Especially since the guy is dead."

Chapter
Sixty-eight

"Dead! How can that be? Sergio said—"

"Aha! Sergio Mandalas was the one who came along and helped you get away. Now it makes sense. He must have also been the one who dropped Juan from a moving vehicle in the front of the LVPD. The cops couldn't identify the black van."

"He promised he'd bring Juan to you. I made him. But he was supposed to be alive."

"He was, barely. He'd sustained injuries, none life-threatening but he'd been beaten all the same. Doctors figure a massive stroke killed him."

"Did you get a chance to question him?"

"Not really. He'd slipped from reality and most of what he said made very little sense. Unless one knew his background, which we did."

"I don't understand."

"According to his file, at the age of ten he'd lost

his mother in an accident and he'd been with her in the car. It took twenty hours for the authorities to find them and she was dead at the scene. By the amount of blood from her wounds, she would have been alive for a lot of the time. And in excruciating pain."

"Was he injured?"

"Cuts and bruises, a broken ankle, nothing massive. The car had flipped so the doors were crushed and wouldn't open. He was trapped inside with her all that time. Before the stroke, he'd babbled on about how she'd begged him to make the pain stop and he'd smothered her with his jacket."

"Oh, God, Trace. How sad. What a terrible thing to have to live with. And then Mary Devin entered his life and had him do the same thing over and over again. No wonder he snapped."

"I know. Have to admit to feeling sorry for the poor son of a bitch in the end. It's a blessing that he's at peace now."

She snuggled into his arms, wanting to stop the shivers that inundated her body. Guilt attacked and it made her cold and sorry and sick. She'd been another user for Juan to deal with. No wonder the poor soul clung to anyone who seemed strong. The women he'd cared about: Mary, Arlene, her and even Dani had all abused his trust.

Trace smoothed her hair back from her face and laid soft kisses on her cheek and then her lips, taking solace and giving it in return.

"I'm so glad we can put this all to rest now, baby. Can't say it ended like I wanted it to. The main thing is—it's over."

She pulled out of his arms. "What do you mean it's over? We don't know who killed Raoul."

Trace's face hardened. Fury began to build and she could see it in the way his hands formed fists and his eyes darkened, becoming cold and scary. "You're kidding me. Juan was the last of the men we needed to arrest at the warehouse that night. You've gotten your justice, right?"

"Not quite."

His voice rose. "What are you talking about? All three men are dead."

"True. But how about the woman who was there? Until I know who she is and what happened that night, I'll be working at the club, asking questions and learning the truth. I want resolutions, Trace."

"Cassi, you have to end this vendetta of yours. It's dangerous. You've been lucky so far, I grant you that. Baby, how long do you figure you can play those cards before you lose the hand?"

"God, Trace, I don't have any answers for you. And that's the whole issue here, isn't it? I need answers. If you want me to sleep at night and be able to live with myself, I can't give up. Not when we're so close."

He groaned. "Baby you're going to be the death

of me yet."

A sinister sensation came over her and she dove into his embrace, needing to block those words from her mind. "Just love me, Trace. Let's forget the world tonight. Let's just be you and me, Trace McGuire and Cassidy Santino, lovers and friends. We can deal with reality tomorrow."

Afterword

Thank you so much for reading the 2nd book in *Her Sweet Revenge Series*, **Justice.**

I loved writing this story and I hope you enjoyed reading it. If so, I would ask you for a favor. Wherever you purchased this book, please take a few minutes and leave an honest review. Authors enjoy hearing that readers like their stories, and hopefully, others will read your words and choose to buy the book because of your sentiments.

My website at **http://mimibarbour.com** now has all my books listed with links to the various publishers to make it easy for you to return to where you bought the book and to find my other work.

While you're there, I'd really appreciate it if you would sign up for my newsletter so I can keep in touch.

http://bit.ly/mimibarbournewsletter

I normally send out newsletters every few months and you have my word that your address will never be shared.

Hugs, Mimi

Resolution

Her Sweet Revenge Series, Book #3
Mimi Barbour
NYT & USA Today Best-selling author

Amazon Universal Link: http://mybook.to/

sweetjustice

***IMPORTANT!! This Series must be read in order – start from Book #1
A gripping story about one woman's quest for justice!

Ever since her brother's murder at the hands of his own gang members, revenge, born of hate, drives Cassidy Santino to make those killers pay.

Recent rumors hint that a female was among the murdering group, which means her search needs to continue. Still working at the bar that doubles as the gang's HQ, Cass walks the nightly tightrope of staying out of the clutches of the she-devil boss/ gang leader, as well as the men who mistake her for being weak, especially the L.A. scumbag who's taken an inordinate dislike to her.

One thing she can't lose – the affections of the detective whose patience with her stubbornness is wearing thin. When he's taken hostage, life goes into an even deeper spiral of conflicts and tension.

Detective Trace McGuire can't bear to watch the love of his life being sucked into the darkness and dysfunction of the Lipstick Club where she bartends. He wants her free of the nightmare. But when he's taken prisoner, how can he help her?

Hell... how can he help himself?

Praise:

"The third book in the series, and they just keep getting better. Mimi Barbour continues the Series with another great story that sees Cassie continuing with her quest to find her brother's killer. The deeper Cassie gets involved with the underworld of Las Vegas while seeking her revenge and resolution, the harder it is for her to stay the sweet girl she once was. Sweet Resolution is another great read by Mimi Barbour that you won't want to miss. Once you begin reading the first page, you won't want to put it down until you have read the whole book. ~ *Reviewed by Laura*

"I have never rated Ms Barbour lower than 5 stars. But this time I am trying not to make it 3 stars. Other authors I have left 1 star for a cliff hanger. That being said she weaves a wonderful story. Her characters come to life. This is quite possibly her best story yet." ~ *Reviewed by Janine*

"What a fantastic third book in this riveting series. We see our heroine develop further both in her own self and her relationship with hot police detective Trace, and we also see some of the supporting characters grow. There are a few plot reveals that will shock you, and there is an almighty cliffhanger at the end! A highly compelling story that has me anxious about the ending." ~ *Reviewed by Bella*

Resolution - Chapter One

Cassidy Santino's life had become complicated, an understatement of huge proportions. Ever since her twin brother Raoul's murder at the hands of *Armas Jóvenes* members, guys in the same gang he'd joined months before, she'd changed from a naïvely shy librarian to a bartender at the sleazy nightclub where that same group hung out. She'd purposely gotten as close to all the lowlifes as possible so she could find her brother's killer.

Revenge had driven her. Money, hidden by Raoul, had funded her. And tenacity fueled the relentless need to make those responsible pay.

Riding her gleaming silver and black Kawasaki NinJarrmono O 250 to the gym where she worked out most days, she ruminated over the last time she'd been on a bike. Had it only been yesterday? God, it seemed unbelievable.

Arlene, the fighter she sparred with at Rusty's Gym, had driven up on her Harley just in time to save her life. If Cassi hadn't been able to leap on the back and get away from crazy Juan and his gun, who knows where she'd be today?

Considering that Arlene had rejected her the first time they'd met, having the girl help her surprised the hell out of Cassi. The incident that came to mind from that day was when they'd fought over Arlene's treatment of Rusty, the old guy who owned Rusty's Gym.

Arlene had been a bitch and Rusty had called her on it. Cassi hadn't intended to intervene. Wouldn't have if Arlene hadn't gotten in her face and if it hadn't turned physical.

By fighting back, using all the tricks she'd been taught over the years of sparring with her brother in their basement gym, she'd set Arlene on her ass. Remembering brought a satisfied smile. No one could disrespect Rusty, not in front of her. She'd lost all her family other than that grouchy old softie, so now he was hers to protect.

Funny thing, once Rusty saw Cassi's skills, he'd begged her to work with him to train Arlene. Turns out, the petulant fighter had huge potential and Rusty wanted to be Arlene's coach.

On her way there now, mind wandering to the recent happenings making her life crazy, she didn't notice the Hummer on her left until they honked and a waving hand motioned her to pull over.

Shit! Sergio Mandalas was not a person anyone could ignore, especially not her. He'd been the second person to help her escape from a killer yesterday.

Wishing the beauty of the morning and the enjoyment she'd experienced from her ride didn't have to be ruined, she swallowed another cuss word and dealt with Sergio.

Being that he was the leader of the *Los Soldados*, rival gang of the *Armas*, it wouldn't do at all to ignore him. In the past, he'd been her brother's friend. Because she'd done him favors, he'd transferred his loyalty to her.

She pulled to a stop, turned off the bike and swung both legs to the side so she could lean her butt on the seat. She removed her helmet and sat it on the handlebars, then fluffed out her hair. Next, she smoothed her jeans and lifted the strap of the black T-shirt that had the tendency to drop off her shoulder on one side.

He approached alone, leaving his bodyguards in the vehicle. She watched him scan the area before he stepped into the open.

"Hey, Sergio."

He cut to the chase. "You hung up on me yesterday."

Scrutinizing his manner to see if this had truly pissed him off or just mildly irritated him, she decided she really didn't care. "Yeah. So?"

Heat rose in his cold eyes, a warning. "So... I wanted to talk to you, Cass. You don't *ever* hang up on me, girl. You dis' me again, and we'll have words."

A serious, no bullshit warning, and it made her change her attitude. She decided only truth would get her out of this pickle, and so she shared.

"Detective McGuire had arrived, and I didn't want him to know we were talking. Sorry, Sergio, but you should know I wouldn't hang up on a friend if I didn't believe it was as much for his sake as mine. The less Trace McGuire knows about our association, the better. Right? If I'm wrong, tell me."

Sergio, face full of tattoos that flowed over his body and even onto his hands, the picture of a gang leader recognizable in any movie, scowled first and then relaxed, his face easing into a grin. "You two getting it on?"

She peeked at him from behind the curtain of her dark hair and let a smile answer him. "And if we are?"

"Damn, girl. You can do better than him. You want we should get together, you just give me a sign."

Cassi laughed. "My friend, you've way too much ego for me. We'd be butting heads every minute."

He winked and nodded. "And you've too much goodness for me. Under all that makeup and sass, Raoul Santino's little sister still exists."

Cassi began to feel nervous, a state she noticed that Sergio tended to create. No doubt it was because during all the time they talked, Sergio never stopped surveying his surroundings, overly cautious because his life depended on it. One of the men from the back of the Hummer, a bald-headed black giant had gotten out and now stood behind the car, his arms folded.

Cassi's nerves flared. Danger lurked, and she felt vulnerable. Being in the open beside this man was putting her life in jeopardy. She sensed his edginess. "You wanted to talk with me?"

"Yeah. You had Billy Duran at your place yesterday."

"Sure, he's an old friend of the family's." Stress jabbed her stomach hard enough to make her belligerent, and it showed in her tone.

Sergio leaned into her space, serious as hell. "You stay away from that bastard, Cass. He's not who you think he is. The man's poison. Drop him."

Cassi reached out and touched his hand. He gently gripped her fingers which gave her the strength to argue. "Sorry, Sergio. No can do. We grew up together. He's family. Billy lived with us while he studied for his law degree. I know he did drugs, lived on the streets. Hell, he was a bad boy. Now he's clean, I can't turn my back on him."

"Cass—"

"Don't ask me. Please, Sergio. He's a link to those old times when dad and Raoul were alive. Like a surrogate brother. I just can't."

"Fuck! You sure know how to make things tough for me, dude. What if I told you Raoul wouldn't like this relationship?"

"How would you know?"

"We talked. Before he joined the gang, we hung out. You know that. He'd be pissed if he knew the truth about the prick."

"Raoul did know about Billy's habit, his drugs and stealing money. But he also tried to help Billy get clean. He wouldn't have given up on him like you're asking me to do."

"Yeah, Cass. He would. Look, just promise me you'll be careful. Don't trust him. There's rumors, none I can prove, but when I get the proof, we'll talk again. Okay?"

She squeezed the fingers she still held before letting them go. "Okay."

From the corner of her eye, she noticed a car slowing down, a window opening, and the barrel of a gun inching forward.

***If you'd like to continue reading this story, click here to my Amazon Universal Link: http://mybook.to/sweetresolution

***All 6 books in Her Sweet Revenge Series are free in Kindle Unlimited.

The Vegas Series

Romantic Suspense at its best
by
New York Times Best-selling author,
Mimi Barbour

AMAZON Universal Link: http://myBook.to/
vegasseries

This sizzling box set for the Vegas Series starts off

where we meet up with hardworking, hard-assed Detective Aurora Morelli. Attempting to arrest a rapist who attacks her colleague then continually thwarts her attempts to bring him to justice—to a horrific nightmare where her new baby is kidnapped—this scrappy detective does everything in her power to control these events. Kai Lawson, a partner she doesn't want, fights against and in the end accepts (in her job and in her bed) is the hero in these first few stories. The bald-headed, purse-carrying hotshot knows just how to pull her crank and the outcome is entertaining. Their blockbuster story will get you totally invested in this series.

In the last three books, along comes Lisa Jordan, a kick-ass kinda gal who loves wearing the shield as a Vegas detective and enjoys the more strenuous aspects of her job. She steps in for a while as Aurora's partner while Kai is MIA. Her story begins here and ends the series as she fights her attraction for wealthy casino owner, Jeff Waters. After one wild night, the charismatic charmer digs his way into her heart and that of the three-year-old nephew in her care. The fact that he leaves her speechless, literally, detracts from his appeal for Lisa since as a self-professed chatterbox, it's the first time ever. On the other hand, everything else about the man is fascinating. She can no more fight her memories than stop herself from rescuing him from two killers holding him hostage in revenge for the mistakes of his father.

~*~*~

Praise for the Vegas series:

"Cops & drama, absolutely loved this series!" ~ reviewed by luvbooks

"Good action and great stories. What a bargain!" ~ reviewed by Johnny Rotten Apples

"Great story lines, wonderful characters!" ~ reviewed by Rachel Larson

"Bloody fantastic!" ~ reviewed by Bernadette Boyce

A word about the author, Mimi Barbour

Author, Mimi Barbour

Mimi is an incredibly busy New York Times, USA Today and award-winning, best-selling author who has nine series to her credit.

She lives on the beautiful east coast of Vancouver Island and fills most of her day with writing and promoting her work. The rest of her time is spent in her garden, doing minimal housework and planning weird meals to ward off starvation.

"The favorite part of my job is meeting the characters from each new book. Creating them the way I want and having them act however I think they should. It's thrilling. Especially when most of my make-believe folks are interesting, witty and in most cases, people I would love to know."

Contact Me:

Write to me, I truly love hearing from my readers!

~ ~

My website: http://www.mimibarbour.com/
Follow me on Twitter, Facebook, Pinterest
Amazon, Goodreads, BookBub, LinkedIn

www.ingramcontent.com/pod-product-compliance
Lightning Source LLC
Chambersburg PA
CBHW030552180626
46816CB00005B/1514